States of Inversion: novella

GRASPING AT GRAVITY

Kallen Samuels

innov@t
PUBLISHING

This is a work of fiction. Names, characters, events and incidents are the products of the author's imagination. Any resemblance to persons, living or dead, or actual events is purely coincidental.

2d9069d7f31da7f1eb4483a9a008d757c2eb70c573c07a4a754ad06f9ba9afcf

ISBN: 978-1-7389011-0-4
Imprint: Innov@t Publishing - https://www.innovat.org

CONTENTS

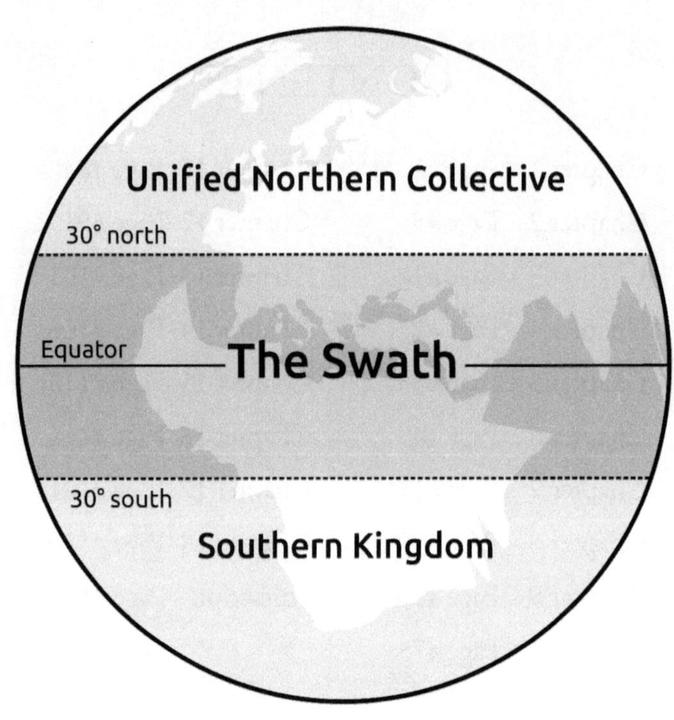

Unified Northern Collective
30° north
Equator
The Swath
30° south
Southern Kingdom

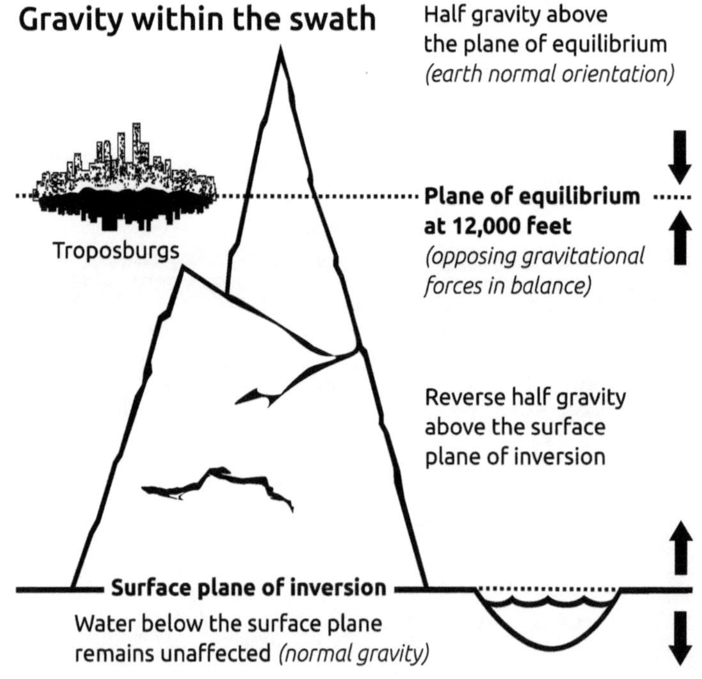

Gravity within the swath
Half gravity above
the plane of equilibrium
(earth normal orientation)
Troposburgs
Plane of equilibrium
at 12,000 feet
(opposing gravitational
forces in balance)
Reverse half gravity
above the surface
plane of inversion
Surface plane of inversion
Water below the surface plane
remains unaffected (normal gravity)

1

Tallow grinned at the satisfying sound of the pneumatic claws digging into the bark and penetrating the cambium of the tree. He inhaled deeply, enjoying the scent of fresh-cut wood.

He needed a few moments to catch his breath after the last series of jumps. Retracting the blades from his right gauntlet, Tallow freed his hand to pound a piton into the sapwood. Clipping a cord from his belt harness to the tree, he anchored his boot spurs, retracted his left gauntlet and leaned back letting the harness support his weight.

He took a moment to admire the new gauntlets. Custom-made to his specifications, the cost nearly emptied the credit in his account, but the devices had already proven their worth. He could travel at nearly twice his normal speed.

Tallow recalled the skepticism on the Vigil's face when he made the request. Most scouts made do with a knife in each hand and their grappling hooks. It seemed an unnecessary extravagance for a young man who should be building credit toward a bride price. Life at the base of the swath came with an expectation to produce offspring for the tribe, and brides were only available from the Luminaries.

Tallow was certainly interested in a bride, but his job was a dangerous one and if he wanted to live long enough to produce offspring, safety was a priority. Caution took time—lost time meant lost credit. He was convinced the gauntlets would enhance his potential to accrue credit without increasing risk. Flint was sending him further abroad, and it took longer to return from a scouting expedition. Tallow needed to find a way to compensate. For every day he was away, he wasn't earning a share of income from the peat harvested by the rest of the tribe in his absence.

His lonely scouting trips in the past had offered plenty of time to refine the concept for the gauntlets. Months worth of crude prototypes littered his cave. They were crafted from broken eating utensils or bent tools he'd claimed from his brothers before they discarded them. Field tests of his last prototype had been satisfying enough that he was confident a properly machined version would perform well. Tallow described what he wanted, handed his prototype to the Vigil and placed his order. It took six long weeks before Vigil Strom finally returned with the professionally machined gauntlets. The results exceeded his expectations. Gleaming steel claws slid smoothly in their sheaths, the blades honed to razor sharpness. The craftsmen had thoughtfully included a tool for maintaining the edge.

That had been a week ago and he'd been experimenting with them ever since. On his current scouting mission, he'd found some tubers in what looked to be part of an ancient cultivated field. Unfortunately, that would only provide a one-time offering and the field wasn't large. A long-term source of a valued commodity was the goal. Ideally, the tribe needed to find more peat or coal to power the forges and vapour engines of the Luminaries. Ore for manufacturing was also in demand, but was much harder to obtain.

Tallow was primarily focussed on finding another peat bog. He hated digging peat, but shifting to coal or minerals would require new tools and that would deplete everyone's credit for years to come. It was bad enough that they needed to look so far abroad. If he found something too remote, it would force the tribe to move their camp. In that event, Vigil Strom would want the sky lift relocated as well. That expense would also affect their credit, but they could do nothing about that potential concern.

Tallow plotted a path through the trees. He'd drifted dangerously close to the limen, the threshold of the swath. It was the point of transition where gravity reversed. Everything within the swath fell toward the heavens, and everything on the other side of the limen fell to earth.

Tallow didn't understand the science behind it, but he'd heard the tales. Five hundred years ago, gravity suddenly reversed within a band that encircled the globe. Everything between the latitudes of thirty degrees on either side of the equator went into a half gravity freerise toward the heavens. Animal life, people, and everything that was unattached took flight with catastrophic consequences. Those who didn't die immediately from flying debris died of exposure while floating helplessly in the ether. Some, lucky enough to be indoors at the time, avoided that immediate fate. In the end, they suffered a worse one — cut off in a world suddenly devoid of provisions, victim to the cruelties of desperate men.

Over hundreds of years, the lack of rainfall and inevitable decay sent a stream of atmospheric flotsam into the troposphere. Somehow, survivors of the catastrophe managed to gather that material and form islands in the sky. Their descendants have lived there ever since.

Occasionally he wondered why the tether tribes remained at the base of the swath. The only answer to that question he'd ever received was that it had always been so. A pragmatic man, Tallow didn't dwell on such things. He'd never seen those islands in the sky, and knowing about them made little difference to the here and now. Life at the base of the swath was difficult enough without daydreaming about some supposed utopia in the clouds. Stumbling about lost in thought was a good way to lose your life. The limen was to be avoided—crossing it from the heavens meant a twelve thousand foot plunge to earth. Crossing it from the earth meant an equally swift freerise through the troposphere where one could expect to drift unnoticed if your heart was strong enough to survive the ascent. He shuddered at the thought of floating helplessly in the ether where a random breeze might blow a survivor across the limen once more, resulting in a second terrifying plunge back down to earth and certain death.

Tallow glanced at the threshold, trying to imagine what it would be like to cross the limen from his current position so close to the surface. They were taught that bones would snap and organs would rupture. The tether tribes maintained a creative debate touting a variety of dire consequences. The fall would be short, but theories abounded about the danger of suddenly transitioning from a half-gravity environment to a full gravity one. Those outcomes were already distressing enough, but for Tallow, the ever-present threat of wild carnivores roaming the wilderness beyond the swath was even worse. Tallow chuckled as he recalled late night conversations around the camp stove. There were many imaginative speculations, but little supporting evidence. Still, it was enough to prevent a reasonable mind from considering a crossing.

Tallow's eyes habitually flicked toward the limen as he moved through the forest. It wasn't difficult to identify the threshold if you knew where to look. Plant life didn't concern itself with borders and provided numerous signs. Inevitably, a tree would produce branches on both sides of the limen, the leaves of some hanging toward the earth and some hanging toward the sky. Perhaps more disorienting was witnessing a flock of birds landing in that same tree—some upside down and some upside right depending on your perspective. Birds seemed indifferent, able to fly in either orientation and transitioning with a simple barrel roll. They often made a game of it as they playfully chased each other back and forth across the threshold.

As a scout, Tallow was attuned to other more subtle signs. Grasses moved in odd ways as breezes forced them across the limen, affected by the contradictory effects of wind and alternating gravitational pull. Flying insects who stumbled through would find themselves darting up and down at the mercy of gravitational flux without the mass to break free. Those and other clues created visible indicators for a trained eye.

Identifying the limen was second nature to anyone raised in its proximity. Nursery rhymes and games entrenched awareness of it from childhood. Regardless, it was part of Tallow's job as a scout to tie colourful ribbons around nearby trees creating more easily spotted markers for his tribe. He did so now as he considered his next jump. The forest had narrowed at this point. No doubt that was how he found himself so close to the limen.

Over centuries, the interior of the swath had become a desert punctuated with water that existed in valleys or underground streams below the plane of inversion. Flora remained confined to riverbanks and lakefronts, creating a spiderweb of tenacious life. The swath also harboured forests along the edge of the limen, spreading roots into areas where rain still fell. Fauna existed in the form of tree-dwelling creatures that were hunted or trapped. Knowing where to dig, one could also unearth small burrowing animals. Aside from providing dietary staples, these green corridors were the only safe means of travel for the tether tribes.

Tallow followed the limen which provided the easiest way to navigate a great distance in a straight line. The true east/west orientation offered a natural compass, simplifying the process of mapping rivers and streams as they crossed his path. He recorded each branching corridor, marking it for future exploration if the direct route proved fruitless. Tallow hoped that would be unnecessary, the tribe had limited time and few resources for exploration.

Leaping earthward in a calculated arc brought him swiftly to the next tree on his path. In those moments between ether and earth, Tallow always experienced the exhilaration that made his lonely journeys bearable. The half gravity of the swath allowed him to travel much further in a jump than would be possible beyond the limen. Tallow often wondered how the Tellusans endured their slow form of travel. One plodding foot in front of the other — feeling weight equivalent to a load of peat even though their arms were empty. Tallow shook the depressing image from his mind as he allowed his fingers to rustle the tall grasses at the apex of his arc. He tucked into a crouch, gauntlets and boot spurs facing the oncoming tree. Blades and spikes sunk into the bark as his muscles absorbed the impact. He took several deep breaths as he hammered in a piton and gathered his safety tether from the previous hitch at his point of departure. The gauntlets helped increase his rate of travel, but the process of relocating his tether was still the slowest part of the process. He hadn't figured out a way to resolve that particular problem.

The voice of Smokey, Tallow's beloved mentor, surfaced in his mind. 'Never fail to plant a piton.' When he became too old to scout, Smokey trained Tallow as his replacement. Smokey had been mentored in turn by a man named Trapper, who designed the spiral piton used exclusively by the Blackspike Tribe. Trapper enjoyed some notoriety until he disappeared while on a scouting mission, never to return. It emphasized the importance of safety measures. Even the most seasoned scout could make a mistake. That loss had a profound impact on Smokey, who had to invent his own techniques to fill in the gaps of his training. He drilled Tallow mercilessly until his protocols were ingrained. "Still," Tallow muttered, "Smokey never had these gauntlets." Tallow glanced at the coiled tether on his right hip. It was long enough to reach between two trees. The gauntlets had proven themselves—maybe he could place a piton every second tree. It would still provide an anchor point.

Tallow quickly tied his tether and chose two candidates for a successive jump. He aimed for a stout bough on the first tree instead of the trunk. It would allow him to launch past on his way to the second objective without coming to a complete stop. If he could master the manoeuvre, it would double his pace. He took a deep breath and launched himself, crouching mid-flight so his hands and feet would land on the branch at the same time. At the moment of impact, he was already springing forward toward the next tree. He had barely left the bough when he saw his mistake. The second tree was diseased, and the bark was loose. He hadn't been able to see that detail from the greater distance. Hands and feet forward, he prayed that his new gauntlets would grant him extra purchase. His claws sank deep—too deep. It was worse than he thought. The tree was beetle infested and the weakened wood crumbled from the impact of his blades. He scrabbled to gain purchase, but spur and blade slid freely as though he were stabbing at loose peat.

Tallow started pinwheeling into freerise—pummelled by branches, his attempts to grab them slipping through his fingers. A moment of panic ensued when he couldn't stop his spin until he recalled something Smokey had once told him. *If you ever find yourself in an uncontrolled gyration, tuck for a moment and then arch your belly into the fall.* Tallow managed to pull out of the spin just as he reached the end of his tether. A vicious jolt jerked his body as the tether pulled tight between harness and piton. The extra length had allowed him to gain too much momentum, and the piton broke free.

Fear gripped Tallow as he considered his impending death. What could he do? *There must be something—wait—the grapple.* He reached for the grappling hook on his other hip and slashed his leg in the process, having forgotten to sheathe the claws of his gauntlets. He ground his teeth in pain as he retracted the blades and pulled the rope from his harness. *Steady, Tallow, you've practised this hundreds of times.* The thought brought little comfort since he'd never practised it while flying through the air as he neared the treetops.

Tallow spun the grapple hook, seeking a target. He would only get one chance before the treetops were beyond reach. He had to make it count. *There!* A kapok tree with a fairly open crown broke through the canopy just to his left. He was out of time and released the grapple—

willing it to connect. Everything slowed to one moment, his life in the balance. The arc was good, the hook was heading toward the tree. Tallow wrapped the end of the tether around his forearm, unwilling to trust the harness alone. The tether crossed a bough as intended and began a centripetal wrap, but before it could complete a full rotation the tether reached its limit. In a state of panic, Tallow yanked the tether as hard as he could to embed the hooks before they had a chance to slip past the bough. Something caught, but he couldn't tell if it was one hook or two. He held his breath and a second later, jerked to a sudden stop.

Tallow was hyperventilating, but only hesitated long enough to alleviate his dizziness—he wasn't out of danger yet. With a slow steady rhythm, he began to pull himself toward the tree. Hand over hand, careful not to allow any slack that might dislodge a precariously placed hook. His arms were burning by the time he placed his own hands on the bough, but he didn't stop until he was at the base of the tree, tied to three pitons—claws and spurs firmly embedded. It was only then that he noticed how close the kapok was to the limen. If his hook had caught on the wrong branch, he would have pulled himself straight across the threshold and plummeted two hundred feet to the earth.

Tallow chose not to dwell on it. It was enough that he was alive. At least that's what he told himself as he hugged the tree a little tighter waiting for his body to stop trembling.

2

"You need to start thinking of your future, Sicily!"

"What do you think I've been doing, Papa?"

Ryo Basurto let out a frustrated huff. "Travelling the world in search of true love isn't a plan."

"Grandma found love with an outsider."

"That was different, he came here. Your grandmother didn't run off looking for someone."

"That's not what this is really about, Papa, and you know it. I don't fit in here. The village views me as an outsider just like they did Grandpa. He looked different too."

"Where would you go? The closest village is seventy miles from here, and it's no larger than this one. The nearest city is over three hundred miles away. How would you get there? You can't travel that distance alone and I'm too old to make such a journey with you."

Sicily held her tongue. She'd heard the arguments before.

"If you marry one of the young men from the village, perhaps you can convince him to leave with you —"

Sicily interrupted. "Look me in the eyes, Papa, and name one person who might consider leaving."

Ryo avoided her gaze.

"The villagers have no imagination or ambition! They're set in their ways."

Ryo lifted his head, indignant. "Is that truly what you think, Sicily? That it didn't take imagination or ambition to settle in this place? The founders of this village had vision and perseverance. They came up with creative ways to establish themselves. The people of Endelton are honest and hard-working. Each generation adding something new, the community growing in size so that one day we might become the kind of city you romanticize. Perhaps you think that vision small, but it's a grand one and I suggest you revise your perspective."

Sicily reddened. "I didn't mean it that way. It's just that—Mama would understand."

Ryo's expression softened as he gathered his daughter into his arms. "I miss her, too, but I'm getting old and I don't want you to be alone when I'm gone."

That was the heart of the matter. Her mother had died giving birth to their second child, their newborn son dying shortly after. The unexpected loss changed her father. Where once he was impulsive and adventurous, now he was fearful and cautious. Her grandparents were no longer alive and the thought of losing his only remaining family paralyzed him. Sicily knew that same fear drove her father to make sure she wasn't alone should he suddenly die.

"Promise me you'll give this more thought."

"I will, Papa."

"I need to get out to the fields. How much longer before the tanning is complete on those three hides? Jenner is asking about them."

"I was going to take two of them off the frames this morning. The third will need a few more days. If you see Jenner in the fields, tell him I can get them to him by week's end."

Ryo kissed Sicily on the forehead and grabbed the lunch she'd packed for him. "I'll see you later."

"Bye, Papa, go easy on your back today."

Sicily turned to the morning's chores, her mind on the conversation with her father. He was only looking out for his little girl, but she wasn't a child anymore. He knew that, of course, or he wouldn't be pushing her to marry.

Somehow, she had to leave this place. She knew her father was right—the village was home to decent folk for the most part, but if she married someone from Endelton, she would remain there for the rest of her life. Even if she found someone willing to consider leaving, the opportunity would never present itself. Something would always get in the way, especially if she had children. She knew that if she became a mother, her priorities would change. That wouldn't be all bad, she wanted children one day, but she wanted to see the world first. Her grandmother had found something more for herself. Sicily just wanted the same opportunity.

Grandfather was an outsider. He came from a place just as small and nowhere near as pleasant. Even so, the stories he told were of a different place with peculiar customs and it filled her mind with a longing to experience everything the world had to offer. Her brows furrowed as she worked at a stain in the trousers she was scrubbing. The fragrance of lavender and lye filled the air—a familiar scent. *I'm so tired of familiar!*

Thoughts drifted to her options. As her father had noted, she couldn't attempt to travel through the wilderness on her own. The risks were simply too great. At a minimum, she needed at least one travelling companion. Any number of events might require an extra pair of arms. Turning an ankle or falling into a ravine were real possibilities. Two could fend off a wild animal or bandit and take turns on night watch. Two could share warmth on a cold night or lift a heavy weight. Perhaps most importantly, two could talk, plan and keep desperation at bay when trouble arose. Sicily could be called hopelessly romantic, impractical, impulsive and many other things, but she wasn't a fool. A larger travelling party would be better, but she'd be lucky to find even one person in

Endelton she could persuade to leave the only home they'd ever known. Somehow she needed to find a willing partner.

Perhaps Adis, the tinker, would have some ideas. His wagon would be coming back through town in a week or so. She had actually approached him in the past and brazenly offered to be his wife if he took her with him. He had smiled indulgently and reminded her that he couldn't fulfill the duties of a husband.

Tinkers were eunuchs by choice, rendering themselves less threatening or prone to the typical compromising temptations. They maintained no relational ties to the world that might create a bias. In exchange, the Guild of Tinkers had unfettered access to the fractured world. They were purveyors of goods, medicines and information. Tinkers were often called upon to store and monitor covenants, armistices and other international agreements. Many governments relied on them to act as couriers, mediators and law enforcement in remote areas. If Sicily were to marry, she'd need Adis, the tinker for their district, to perform the ceremony. He'd also be responsible for submitting the official records when he passed through a city with a courthouse.

Unfortunate, Sicily thought for the hundredth time. It would be the fastest and safest way for her to travel. Bandits and cutthroats understood that tinkers were off limits, despite the tempting wares they transported. Few would risk having a bounty placed on their heads by the military, who made gruesome examples of those they hunted down. Witless thugs inevitably tried, but learned very quickly just how well trained the tinkers were in the combative arts, not to mention the extensive arsenal within their armoured wagons. Even if a band of brigands were successful in subduing a tinker, they would never lay hands on the treasures locked within. No one had ever succeeded in penetrating a tinker's cart without destroying its contents.

Perhaps Adis knew someone from another town who felt as she did—then she'd only have to travel alone for a short time. Adis might even escort her part of the way. Tinkers were known to offer that service from time to time if an individual could provide their own transportation and supplies. Lomar Romero had done that very thing two seasons ago. He'd travelled to a remote village and procured some expensive equipment so he could expand his business. She'd have to remember to ask Adis about his fees. Unfortunately, if she went that route, it also meant she'd need to buy a mount. It wasn't the most feasible option, so she moved on to other possibilities.

Sicily stood from her work. The only thing left on her list was the milk deliveries. She always left that errand for last. It meant she would run into other women her age—women who had shunned her for years. Sicily had inherited the foreign attributes of her outsider grandfather. As children, the other girls teased her relentlessly because she looked different and played with the boys. Her father said they would grow out of it, but it only got worse as they matured and the perception of her *different* features shifted to exotic and alluring. It wasn't that the other girls were unattractive, it was just that they all had a sameness about them. They didn't try to hide their jealousy or resentment and Sicily's isolation continued. If even one of them had befriended her, maybe she wouldn't be as eager to leave. *No, I'd still feel the pull, but this makes it easier to consider leaving.*

Maybe she could use the deliveries as an opportunity to feel them out and see if any of them had dreams of travel or life in the big city. Alisha was known for the occasional flight of fancy, and her house was the first stop.

When Alisha answered the knock at the door, her expression turned sour. "Oh, it's you."

Sicily put on a friendly face. "Just delivering the milk. Here you go. How are things? Any travel plans?"

Alisha shook her head in disgust.

"Is there a problem? Is something wrong with the milk?"

"You think you're better than us, don't you?"

"Excuse me?"

"Are you still preoccupied with foreign lands? Ever since you were a child, you'd go on and on about how great your grandfather was. You were always hanging out with the boys, telling them tales of your grandfather's adventures, how one day you'd go on adventures of your own. Even back then you had the boys wrapped around your baby finger."

Sicily choked at the accusation. "What? I only played with the boys because all of you ignored me. I didn't have any other options!"

"If that's true, then why are you leading them on now that they're young men? Always waggling your backside, drawing their eyes, flaunting your looks."

"I do *not* waggle! I'm not even interested in them. All they ever talk about is sowing, harvesting or calving season." Sicily truly couldn't understand their narrow range of passions. The tinker carried news from around the world and all they were interested in was the latest tools he offered. They seemed to think life here would always remain untouched—protected by a little bubble of anachronism.

Alisha raised a brow. "So they're not good enough? You're better than them?"

"That's not what I said! I just meant that I'm not trying to woo them."

"If you're not flirting, then why do they flock to you like bees to a flower? Ten of us could be standing in a room and they'd walk right past us to get to you."

"That's not fair, Alisha. You just make them uncomfortable. They don't know how to act around you. It's easy for them to approach me because they've known me their entire lives and just see me as a friend."

Alisha huffed. "Are you really that naive or are you fishing for a compliment? Very well, if that's what you need to hear, then I'll say it. You're a beautiful woman, Sicily, and I think you know it. The rest of us can't compete, and we're getting tired of it. You need to grow up and the men do too."

Sicily was in a state of shock. She'd put up with their ostracism for a lifetime and now they blamed her because they weren't getting enough male attention? *Unbelievable!*

"How is it that you hold me responsible for the actions of the men? Are you telling me that if a man ignores you when I'm not around, it's still my fault?"

Alisha didn't back down. "Why don't you just decide already? I hear Lomar has offered a bride price to your father."

"Lomar!" Sicily sputtered, "Would *you* marry Lomar?"

Lomar Romero had a cruel streak. She'd seen him do terrible things to small animals when he was a child. Lomar made her uncomfortable and she didn't trust him at all. He'd managed to build a very profitable business sharpening tools and kitchen knives which seemed disturbing considering his character. She knew he'd been talking about starting a family and had expressed an interest in her, but she didn't know he had approached her father. *How could Papa have kept this from me? Is that why he brought up marriage this morning?* Would he listen to her concerns about the man? She could imagine her father saying, "People change, Sicily, and that was a long time ago." She didn't think her father would force her into a marriage she opposed, but the bride price must have impressed him or why keep it secret?

Alisha sighed like someone beaten down by life. It struck Sicily how much older she appeared as a result.

"I'm going to spell this out for you, Sicily. This town has only so many men. Whether you're intentionally leading them on or not, they're all infatuated with you. Each of them dreams they'll be the one you choose. They won't give up hope while you remain unmarried. Until that happens, the rest of us are invisible. It's bad enough that whomever we end up marrying will probably be fantasizing about you for the rest of their days, but it's all we have."

Alisha's voice had been increasing in volume, and faces were peering out of the neighbour's windows. "None of us are growing any younger, Sicily. Stop playing games and choose!"

The door slammed shut on Sicily's face. The rest of her deliveries, while silent, were equally hostile. Alisha must have turned them all against her—again.

I guess I can't anticipate a female travelling companion. At least not from around here.

Sicily considered her male friends and couldn't think of one that had ambitions beyond Endelton. It galled her to think that she may have no choice but to settle and make the best of it. She knew the men to be hard-working, generous and kind. Any of her childhood friends would make a good husband if it came to that. In time, she supposed, she could learn to love whomever she married, yet it didn't seem right. That's not the way it was supposed to happen, was it? Why was life so unfair?

Sicily wondered what life would have been like if her brother had survived. Would he have helped her leave this place? At least she'd have had someone to stand up for her—someone who shared her history and understood what it felt like to be unique. It was a pleasant fantasy that diffused her anger over Alisha's accusations, but only briefly.

She still had some time before the men returned from the fields. It was a beautiful day, so she decided to walk to the limen and blow off some steam. She could pick some berries for dessert. *Maybe I'll visit Grandfather's stone.* It was a bad idea that would likely make things worse—ruminating over her predicament at her grandfather's monument only intensified her desire to travel. Still, a walk would do her good.

Weather was often unpredictable near limen, but today the cloudless sky allowed the sun to shine as a rival to her dark mood. The gentle breeze and the birdsong were also at odds with her countenance. She was so preoccupied that she didn't remember arriving among the bushes. It wasn't until she pricked her finger on a thorn that she noticed where she was and that her bucket was already half full. Judging by the heavy sensation in her stomach, more berries had found her mouth than the bucket. She wiped self-consciously at her lips, imagining a mess, then shook her head at the thought, knowing no one was around to see.

A loud crack interrupted her thoughts, and her fingers stilled while reaching for a berry.

What was that? Looking around for a large animal, Sicily crouched and picked up her walking stick. It was probably just a ruminant she felt safer with something solid in her hands. Her back facing the limen, Sicily made a slow turn. Nothing appeared to be approaching. She heard more rustling and realized it was coming from behind her. Sicily breathed a sigh of relief, nothing on the swath side of the limen was a threat. *Wait, that can't be right. No large animals exist in the swath.* The next sound she heard was a very human yelp high in the branches.

Sicily looked up and clamped a hand over her mouth as she spotted a flailing man rapidly rising through the treetops. Just when she thought all hope was lost, he spun a grappling hook, caught a tree and pulled himself to safety. She watched in silence as he climbed down the tree and tethered himself to the base, not more than ten feet away from her. He was the most breathtaking man she had ever seen.

3

Sicily froze in place, unwilling to disturb anything about the moment as she analyzed the situation. The man in front of her looked to be about her age or slightly older. Leather boots sheathed his legs to the knee and gauntlets to his elbows. A harness crossed his torso. A loincloth, and what looked like vines knotted into netting, covered the remainder of his body. She imagined it provided protection from tree branches while allowing cool air to flow through.

She felt her face heat as she realized how much skin she could see. He had the familiar build of those from the tether tribes—tall, with fine bones from a lifetime spent in half gravity. Not that he looked frail, he was broad-shouldered and every inch of his body displayed chiselled muscle glowing with a sheen of sweat from his recent exertion. Having watched him climb to safety, she already knew his reactions were whiplike and precise. His movements were lithe and surprisingly quick. She wondered if he could maintain that in full gravity. Just for a moment she worried he might cross the limen. He wouldn't have far to fall from his current position. The possibility sent a thrill up her spine and a part of her hoped he would. Without really thinking, she took a step forward.

The vision came to life, head rotating as her movement caught his attention. She heard a clicking of beads from the rows of tight braids woven into his long blonde hair. Sicily took several steps closer, but stopped when his eyes locked onto hers. *What am I doing?*

She inhaled sharply as she saw his face. He had the enthralling features she only encountered while dreaming. Granted, variety was limited in her village, but this was closer to an ideal than she'd seen so far in her life and she felt a little wave of desire.

His green eyes stared into her own until she broke his gaze. His muscles coiled—whether to attack or flee she wasn't certain. She'd only ever heard of one instance where a tribesman crossed the limen, so she assumed it was the latter. She wasn't ready for him to leave, so she held her palms out in a gesture of peace. He relaxed visibly and then turned his body so he was no longer upside down from her perspective. He gathered his braids with a cord and continued to stare at her in silence. She grew self-conscious and touched her lips. "Do I have berry juice all over my face?"

Just great, Sicily, that's your opening question?

He seemed startled by her voice, but she decided to push on. "My name is Sicily Basurto." She half turned and pointed in the direction of her home. "I live in the village of Endelton a few miles in that direction. I didn't realize tether tribes lived in the vicinity."

Cocking his head, a puzzled expression creased his brow at her mention of tether tribes. "What do you know of my people?" He paused and then added, "Your face is free of berry juice."

"So you can talk. I was beginning to wonder. Do you have a name?"

He fell silent again and his gaze shifted from her face, lingering as he slowly took in the rest of her form. She surprised herself by straightening to her full height. It was a completely uncharacteristic feeling, but for some reason she enjoyed his attention.

"You act like you've never seen a woman before."

Realization struck her. "How stupid of me. Of course you haven't. Men of the tether tribes meet a woman for the first time on their wedding day and then only briefly."

He flinched at her comment but continued to stare.

"Do you like what you see?" Sicily made a slow turn as his eyes remained riveted on her. It was an ignoble display, but she felt powerful—her own little rebellion against the expectations of society. It was a guilt-free act seen by no one who would judge, or so she thought, until the words of her father emerged to confront her regardless. "Remember, Sicily, it's what you do when you know your actions will never be discovered that defines who you are."

"My name is Tallow—From the Blackspike Tether Tribe."

"Tallow? As in animal fat?"

Tallow let out a bark of laughter. "No, the tribe thought my hair looked the colour of a tallow candle."

"I'm still stuck on the animal fat image. Can I just call you Tal?"

"If it's typical for your culture to shorten names, then that will be acceptable. Shall I call you Sis?"

"No!" Sicily shuddered. "No—don't call me sis. That would feel—weird."

Tallow shrugged, confused by her outburst.

Sicily shifted the conversation. "I saw you recover from freerise. That was impressive. I thought you were a goner and then you did that grappling thing after you'd already passed the treetops. I wouldn't have believed it possible, yet I saw it with my own eyes. Is that a typical manoeuvre among your people?"

Tallow frowned, looking as though he wished she had asked any other question, then sighed. "No, that was the result of a foolish mistake. I could have died."

"That would have been a waste." *Sicily! What's wrong with you?* "Um, I mean I'm really glad you're alive, uh, didn't die." Sicily's eyes caught on an exposed hip, and she noticed the gash on Tal's leg. "You're injured!"

Tallow waved it off. "It's nothing."

"Don't compound foolishness. It could get infected. We need to dress it." Sicily looked around for something suitable to use as dressing and had a six-inch strip torn from the hem of her knee-length skirt before recalling that she had no way to reach him. She shook her head. "I'm sorry, I just realized I can't help you from here."

Tallow reached into his belt and pulled out a small jar containing some kind of crawling insects. He answered her unasked question. "Biting ants." He removed one from the jar and held his wound closed as he placed the jaws of an ant on either side of the cut and pinched off its body after it bit into his flesh. When he'd completed his task, a rudimentary line of sutures sealed his wound. He slathered a pungent ointment over the injured area, plucked a few leaves to use as a bandage and tied it off with a leather thong. The whole process was hypnotic and it took a moment for her to notice he was staring at her again. She redirected his attention with another question.

"Did you say your tribe lived nearby?" She didn't know why she was treating this encounter like a casual conversation. A few hours ago, she was worrying about the dangers of bandits on a journey. Now, here she was talking to a total stranger as though he was just a friendly neighbour. Her eyes drifted to his gauntlets. When she first approached, he'd had his gleaming claws embedded into a tree. She shook her head. It wasn't the same. The limen stood between them. *You know that a tribesman crossed that barrier once before.* Sicily reconsidered the strength flowing through Tal's frame. He could obviously overpower her. *What if other tribesmen are nearby?* She suddenly became very interested in hearing the answer to her question.

"I'm far from home."

Sicily felt her tension easing.

"I'm on a scouting mission for the tribe."

Her suspicion spiked. She'd told him where she came from and pointed out the direction to her village.

"What are you scouting?"

"My tribe digs peat for the Luminaries. The bog is depleting. We need to find a new source."

Sicily's fears evaporated. He wasn't a threat. He served his tribe in the same mundane way that she worked for her village—two people who happened to cross paths in the performance of their duties. Strangers from two different cultures, equally curious about one another. The very type of adventure she imagined—minus the attraction factor. Not that she was complaining.

"What's it like to live as a slave to the Luminaries?"

Tallow stiffened. "I'm not a slave."

"You said that you dig peat for the Luminaries. I believe you were referring to the founders of the Tropos Archipelago."

Tallow appeared confused.

Sicily pointed to the sky. "The Aerish. You know, the people living on the islands in the sky above the swath."

Tallow nodded in understanding.

"Luminaries..." Sicily sniffed derisively. "No one uses that pompous self-appointed appellation outside of the swath. Just because the Aerish are physically elevated, doesn't mean they're above us in every other sense of the word."

"I know nothing of their politics or yours. What I do know is that I'm not a slave."

"Yet you wear a leash and refer to the Aerish with a title—that gives them power over you. Do they pay you for your labour?"

"It's not a leash! It's a safety tether. We live our lives as we wish. Digging peat is a way to earn credit in exchange for goods offered by the Luminaries." Tallow unsheathed the blades on his gauntlet. "I used some of my credit to have these gauntlets built by luminary craftsmen. We don't have the facilities to produce such things on our own. Transactions like that are merely trade. In all other things, we provide for ourselves."

"So you're saying that without the Aerish, your people would get along just fine?"

"They're called Luminaries, and yes."

"They hold nothing over you?"

"Nothing."

"Then why have you never seen a female before?"

"It's not like that. The base of the swath is a dangerous place for women, children, old men and the infirm. The Luminaries provide a safe place for them to live. Some of the credits we earn go toward their support. When the young men of my tribe reach the age for marriage, they are paired with a wife. Our wives are taken to safety where they give birth to our children. If the child is male, he returns to the tribe once he's old enough to grasp a tether. Our wives prepare a home for the day of hoisting when we retire from our work and rejoin them in the sky. Our daughters remain with their mothers until they're of age to pair with a young man from the tribe."

"Is that what they told you?"

"That is the way it has always been and is all we know. Why would I think otherwise?"

"Can you choose your spouse or the time of marriage?"

Tallow snapped back in irritation. "Can you?"

That comment cut a little too close to home. Sicily's options for a husband were limited and her father was pushing her to marry before she felt ready. Considering Lomar had offered a bride price, wasn't he treating her nuptials like a transaction in a similar manner? Sicily changed the subject. "At what age does a tribesman retire?"

"It varies, but generally the hoisting occurs in the thirtieth season following a spousal joining."

Sicily looked aghast. "So young?"

"You would have us wait longer to rejoin our wives?"

"Listen to me, Tal, there's no reward. The Luminaries are using you."

Tallow's visage darkened. "How could you know anything about my people or their ways? Who are you to judge or make such accusations?"

"I know more than you think."

"Or much less than you imagine. Where do you get your information?"

"The tinker."

"What's a tinker?"

"Not what, who. The tinker is a travelling salesman. He also carries news of the outside world and entertains the community with stories."

"So you purchase items and get your information from an outside source as well? Someone you rely on for certain things?" Tallow gave Sicily a hard look, and she felt her face heat at the comparison.

"It's not like that, Tal. I learned this from a tribesman who bore witness of events following a hoisting ceremony. The tribe said its farewell to the elders of their group, then they set off for their daily work. This man, the scout, had left something behind and returned. He saw the older ones clipped to a ground tether that led to the sky lift. They were heading to their reward. When they were in the open, half the distance to the lift, the Aerish cut the tether."

Tallow had a horrified expression on his face. "No! You're lying!"

"It's the truth. That scout fled and never returned. He crossed the limen and settled among the Tellusans."

"I don't believe you. Who told you this? Your tinker? You've already said he's a storyteller. This is just a myth to malign the tether tribes."

"It's not a myth and I can prove it."

"Why are you saying these things to me? We've only just met. Have I wronged you somehow?" Tallow squeezed his eyes shut. He took several deep breaths to calm himself and looked directly at Sicily, his eyes full of disappointment. "I need to go. The tribe is waiting for me."

Sicily felt a stab of guilt. She'd only meant to warn him, but instead had damaged something new and tenuous. "Wait. When will you return? I'd like to see you again."

Tallow turned sad eyes her way. "Why? So you can continue your attack on our culture? So you can call me a fool for living the only life I've ever known?"

"Tallow, no—please. I didn't mean to hurt you. I shouldn't have said those things. I'm sorry, it was wrong. Please, don't leave in anger."

Sicily could see the struggle behind his eyes. Anger and frustration were clearly present, but also curiosity and a longing for something more. She recognized the sentiment well enough.

"I need to resupply and then I will be continuing my exploration in this direction. I should be back at this point in about two weeks' time. I make no promises, but you can look for me then." Tallow extended his claws and carved three horizontal lines across the tree where he clung. "When I return, if I'm willing to meet, I will carve another three lines below these. If after three weeks, you still only see three marks, it means you'll never see me again."

Following that proclamation, Tallow scaled the trunk with astonishing speed, leaped toward the ground and rose again to land on a distant tree. He didn't look back as the second jump took him out of sight.

As Sicily stood there alone, she had a terrible revelation about the longing of her heart. The adventures of her grandfather were less important to her than the true love found by her grandmother. Tal stirred feelings she'd never experienced before. He was attractive, but he was also intelligent and curious about the world around him. She wasn't naive enough to think that he shared an interest in her, but he'd helped her to understand what it was like to have those feelings. She might find them again with another, as close as one village away. She'd been chasing a dream of adventure with no promise of fulfillment. Now, she had a better understanding of what she was truly searching for.

And if he was the one, Sicily? What then?

"Then I've made a terrible mistake," she whispered.

His final words burned into her heart.

"... You'll never see me again."

Sicily sank to her knees from the burden her predicament placed on her shoulders.

4

Sicily finally relented and agreed to meet with Lomar just to end her father's relentless nagging. She regretted it from the moment a carriage arrived at her home to pick her up. She was chauffeured to Lomar's estate where they shared a meal. She begrudgingly admitted to herself that she enjoyed the imported wine and appreciated the exotic spices used to prepare the venison—Lomar's embellished retelling of the hunt for this particular beast, decidedly less so. While the meal was enjoyable, Lomar had outdone himself with dessert. Sicily couldn't imagine how he got his hands on chocolate. It was a rare treat and she couldn't hide the pleasure it elicited. Lomar was smiling broadly, imagining he had scored some major points in his favour. Sicily cursed her weakness.

Sicily spent the remainder of the afternoon touring Lomar's considerable holdings. The house was larger than most in Endelton, the yard well manicured and the outbuildings well kept. Several mounts trotted up to the fence when they neared, looking for a treat. Everything had its place and understood its role. Even the canines were well mannered, quietly walking at Lomar's side and sitting at attention whenever he stopped to point out a feature. Most villagers would be impressed, but Sicily knew Lomar was a big fish in a small pond and was convinced he would be less impressive in a large city. He droned on about his success and his contributions to the community, endeavours clearly a lot bigger in his mind than anyone else's.

Lomar's calculated display of wealth was obvious and pretentious. The inane conversation didn't help his bid, although he seemed convinced otherwise. Sicily played along for what she considered a polite length of time. *Papa can't accuse me of failing to give it a chance.*

Finally, she'd had enough. *If I don't leave now, I'll start making sarcastic remarks.* "I'd like to thank you for a pleasant afternoon, Lomar, but I should be getting back. I have quite a few chores I'm behind on. I'm sure you have business to attend to as well."

Lomar appeared confused. "Your father assured me that you were free of responsibilities for the day."

"Is that so?" Sicily scowled. It was time to get things out into the open. "Lomar, may I ask why you've invited me here? You've never done so in the past."

"I thought it important that we get to know each other, all things considered."

Sicily raised an eyebrow and waited for more.

"Didn't your father tell you?

"Tell me what, exactly?"

"That I asked for your hand in marriage."

Sicily knew about the bride price, but her father still hadn't shared that piece of information with her. "He made no mention of having discussed any arrangements with you. My father is well aware of my feelings regarding marriage and I doubt he has agreed to anything without my acceptance."

Lomar seemed to realize he'd made a tactical error. "I apologize, Sicily. I was unaware he hadn't spoken with you yet. Regardless, you're here now and I'm more than happy to discuss matters with you. I've worked hard to establish myself —." Lomar held his arms out and slowly turned to indicate his estate. "—and now it's time for me to settle down and start a family. It's time to share this with someone."

"Lomar, didn't it occur to you that it might be wise to gauge a woman's interest before planning a wedding?"

"I don't understand." Lomar looked genuinely perplexed. "I'm attractive and successful. I can take very good care of you, Sicily."

Sicily held her tongue at that particular declaration, but her thoughts were far less charitable.

"This isn't a business transaction, Lomar. I don't need someone to take care of me and I have plans of my own."

Lomar was nodding as if he understood. "Yes, your father mentioned that you wanted to travel. I can offer that to you as well. In fact, I have a trip planned to Coltram City in two years' time."

"Lomar, I don't know how to say this politely... I'm not interested in marriage right now. Even if I were, I wouldn't choose you."

A vein began to throb in Lomar's neck. "This is not the way to win my favour, Sicily. I thought you had more sense than that."

"Excuse me? I'm not trying to win your favour or anything else for that matter."

"Who else would you choose? Hugo? He's half your height and ugly as the peccaries he raises. Joaquin? The man doesn't have two coins to rub together. Luis? That simpleton will never amount to anything. The Marin brothers may as well be married to their orchards and wine presses—choose either one of them and you'd never travel anywhere. And in case you hadn't noticed, they sample far too much of their product."

Sicily was fuming. "Those are friends of mine, each of them kind and generous. Virtues you seem to lack. Your arrogance is astonishing and far uglier than Hugo or his peccaries. If you believe your imagined superiority is impressing me, you're sorely mistaken."

Lomar's anger matched her own. "Your self-righteous indignation is misplaced! Everyone in town knows how vain you are. The womenfolk despise you and the unmarried men your age can't support you. This is a small village, Sicily, I'm the only real choice you have, but you're not my only option. Quit being foolish and get over yourself."

If one more man calls me foolish, so help me... "I'm sure that Alisha would be happy to receive your attention. You don't even need to ask her father for her hand. I'll give you my blessing instead. You two deserve each other. I don't need help from either of you and I can take care of myself, thank you very much."

"How?"

"What did you say?"

"I asked you, how? How will you take care of yourself? I really don't think you've thought this through. What will you do when your father dies?"

Now it was Sicily's turn to look perplexed. "What a silly question. I'll do what I've always done. Do you think our farm runs on its own while my father works in the public fields?"

"Why do you think your father works in the public fields instead of helping you?"

Sicily hadn't given it much thought. It had been that way since her mother died. At first she thought that he needed to get away from reminders of what he'd lost. Eventually, it just became the new norm.

"I suppose he likes to save up some extra money for a rainy day."

"Sicily, your father is deep in debt. He barely makes enough in the fields to cover his interest payments. It's getting worse every year as he finds it more difficult to put in full hours. On those days when he has to stop early because of his back, he visits the gambling house. Hoping to gain something there, he ends up losing more for his efforts."

"It's not true. He's never mentioned anything about financial difficulties."

"No? You were quick to point out that your friends are kind and generous, but you didn't include me. Apparently, you're unaware that I secured your father's debt. If it had not been for my help, you would have lost the farm years ago. I've made several interest payments on his behalf in the years since."

"That—it—you..." Sicily was at a loss for words. How could her father have kept this from her?

Seeing her uncertainty, Lomar pushed his advantage. "When your father dies, the house, the land, the fields and everything he owns will fall to me. You will have no inheritance. So I ask you again, Sicily, how will you take care of yourself?"

Sicily felt like she needed to sit down, but she didn't want Lomar to think he'd achieved some kind of victory. She willed her legs to stop trembling. The farm, her life, all of it was an illusion. She couldn't stay in Endelton, but lacked the means to leave. She couldn't care for her father or herself. She had nothing and no one. Even her father had let her down.

"If we were to marry, I would take care of both you and your father."

"You planned this! You're evil!"

"No, Sicily, I'm not evil, I'm just a businessman. Your father approached me, not the other way around. I happened to be one of the few people with the resources to help. I wasn't even considering marriage at the time. Quite frankly, it's a little egotistical of you to assume I've been coveting you for years. You're misinterpreting my current pragmatism, not to mention my generosity. I did your family a huge favour by securing your father's debt, I didn't *need* to offer a bride price."

There it was—that word again. Her *price*. She knew that wasn't the original purpose of a bride price, but it felt like a valuation anyway. Sicily felt like a trapped animal, or perhaps a hunted one. The way Lomar was looking at her, she couldn't help feeling like she was venison for a future meal. The smug grin on his face looked sinister despite his assurances to the contrary. Sicily turned and ran.

***

It took Sicily an hour to walk home. When she arrived, her father was waiting.

"How did it go?" he asked.

"How did it go? How did you imagine it would go? You know how I feel about Lomar! Did you really think I would return with love in my

31

eyes?"

Ryo shrugged. "I thought if you gave him a chance, you might change your mind about him."

Sicily stared at her father until he began to squirm. "When were you going to tell me?"

Ryo evaded her glare. "Tell you what?"

"Enough! You've been hiding things from me—lying to me for years!"

Ryo wilted.

"Papa, why didn't you tell me we were in debt? I could have helped. I could have found employment."

"It's not your job to take care of me. I'm supposed to take care of you."

"By going further and further into debt? What was your plan? To keep it a secret until we both found ourselves on the street begging for food?"

"You won't end up on the street. You're young and beautiful. You'll make a wonderful partner for someone. You'll be fine. I'll face the consequences of my mistakes on my own."

"And what about Lomar's bride price? When were you going to share that piece of information? How could you even consider making marriage arrangements without consulting me? You know how I feel about this."

"What would you have me do? I couldn't refuse to consider his request after everything he's done for me. He's a very generous man, Sicily. He has helped us out for years without asking anything in return. I thought you might see a different side of him if you got to know him like I know him. What harm is there in testing the waters? Besides, no one else has requested your hand."

Curiosity got the better of her. "What was the bride price, Papa?"

Ryo looked sheepish and Sicily began to wonder just how little she was worth. "Papa?"

"He offered to cancel my debt."

"The interest you owe him?"

"No, all of it."

Sicily was shocked, then flattered and finally outraged. "You were going to sell me to pay off your debt?"

"It's not like that!"

"Papa!" Sicily shook her head. "It's exactly like that! You've been trying to convince me to consider Lomar ever since he gave his bride price."

"I wasn't going to try forcing you into anything."

"That's besides the point. It's one thing to approach a benefactor for a loan and another thing altogether to offer someone else in payment."

"You're free to say no. It was always your choice." Ryo countered.

"Truly, Papa? If I don't marry Lomar to pay for your mistakes, we both end up homeless on the day when you can no longer work in the fields. What kind of choice is that? Is that what you want?"

"No, of course not."

"So you admit that you want me to marry Lomar."

Ryo shrugged. "I know this looks bad, Sicily, but I'm just trying to be practical. I've failed you. I admit it. At this point, nothing I do will regain title of the farm. I have nothing to bequeath you. You've said yourself that you're not interested in any of the men in this village, but as you now know, you lack resources with which to leave. Lomar is one of the wealthiest men in the village. He's willing to marry you, and he can provide a very comfortable life. It may not be what you wish, but it's what's available to you."

Ryo paused as he picked up a framed picture of Sicily's mother. "We don't always get what we want. Sometimes life turns out very different than we imagine and we have to make the best of it."

Sicily's temper flared. "You don't get to use that card, papa! This isn't one of the games you play at the gambling house. You weren't the only one who suffered when Mama died. My life changed, too. I had to grow up quickly and take over the household while you were off gambling your earnings. It turns out I've been taking care of us both and paying for your mistakes this whole time! You don't get to play the victim. Not anymore."

Sicily stared at him until he turned his eyes to the floor. "No more lies, Papa. Look me in the eyes and tell me. When you were offered the bride price, when you encouraged me to consider Lomar, were you thinking only of my welfare or were you thinking about paying off your debt?"

Sicily waited patiently, but Ryo refused to look at her. "That's what I thought. I need to take a walk."

Sicily slammed the door as she stepped out into the cool evening, leaving her father to his misery.

5

Tallow sat cross-legged on the skyward side of his cave, grateful once more for the perk his scout status afforded him. Outside of a cave, tribesmen remained tethered so they wouldn't float away while distracted or sleeping. Sketching was difficult when tethered and the stability of sitting on the broad surface within the cave made the pastime far more pleasant. Tallow couldn't get Sicily out of his head. He was attempting to sketch her from memory.

All the young men of the tribe heard descriptions of females from their brothers who had experienced a wedding night, but they really had no context other than the physiology and mating practices of animals in the forest. Those mental images were a poor substitute for the real thing.

Tallow had been stunned into silence when he laid eyes on Sicily. She was nothing at all like what he had imagined. He understood why the newly wed men in his tribe found it so difficult to put their experience into words. With deft strokes, he did his best to capture Sicily's likeness while she was still fresh in his mind. Apart from the most obvious differences which were certainly pleasing to his eyes, many subtle distinctions stood out in his mind. The curvature of the spine, the flowing transitions from chest, to waist, to hips. Even the musculature of arms and legs were unique. Yet it was more than that. The way she moved was mesmerizing. The curves and musculature seemed designed to hypnotize prey.

Having grown up wrestling the brothers of his tribe, he was very familiar with the range of motion for joints and limbs but he couldn't reconcile that knowledge with the differences in his sketches. It seemed somehow like Sicily would break if he used those same wrestling holds on her. Perhaps that was part of the hypnotic spell—to trick a man into a dangerous miscalculation. Regardless, any thoughts of wrestling with Sicily were lacking aggression, replaced with a desire to explore. It was ... both threatening and pleasing at the same time.

Invariably, Tallow found himself returning to memories of her face, spending far more time on those details of his sketch. Her long black hair fell free across her shoulders, framing her visage. Her jawline and brow had sharp definition, yet curved in a way that did as much to soften her features as other curves softened her figure. Even the eyebrows had an upward curve instead of the far straighter slash across the more prominent brow of a typical man. Everything about her face was a petite version of the masculine features he was familiar with. Most captivating of all was her eyes—an emerald green that made his heart skip a beat when he looked into them. He could only manage it for a short time before he had to look away. The shimmer of her hair would catch his attention and draw his eyes down past her shoulders to linger, but only for a moment before his gaze returned to those eyes and started the process all over again. She appeared at times uncomfortable with his stare, but also seemed to encourage it. It was all very confusing.

His mind drifted back to their conversation. Sicily's voice caught him off guard. It had a musical aspect to his ears—intonations that carried a quality he found comforting. Tallow had no memory of his mother, taken from her at a very young age, but he thought perhaps the comfort he felt was a vestige of that long-lost connection.

Then came her words. They started out as questions and turned into blades. Sharp criticism about his culture and an attitude of superiority, like she knew the ways of the tribe better than he did. It was irritating and belittling. Her body language was inviting while her words put up barriers every bit as effective as the limen. When he ended their exchange and left her behind, it was with conflicted emotions. He didn't get very far before doubling back, but instead of announcing his presence, he remained hidden. He wanted to have a more positive memory of their encounter in case they never met again. It seemed like the best way to guarantee that would be to avoid verbal communication, so he watched in silence.

That decision only served to confuse him more. Thinking herself alone, she fell to the ground as if defeated by the encounter. Was she genuinely sorry to see him go? He hadn't believed her when she said she was sorry for her words, yet she seemed truly mournful as he watched from his perch. Was she cruel or caring? She had seemed stricken by his wound and wanted to dress it, suggesting that she didn't want him to suffer harm. It made no sense to him and she remained there for a lot longer than he would have expected from someone with a hardened heart. Tallow had almost gone to her then, longing to wipe away her tears—to protect her. She looked so vulnerable. Reality kicked in when he recalled the limen obstructing his path. He couldn't cross it to comfort her. Every tribesman's education included exhortations on the danger—bones would shatter, organs would burst. Those who lived in the half gravity of the swath couldn't handle the strain of a full gravity environment. Tallow chastised himself for his foolish thoughts about a woman he'd only just met. He shook his head as he considered the alternative. A female crossing the limen would be sent to the Luminaries to protect her from the dangers of the swath. He could see no way for them to be together even if they'd had the time to forge a friendship. It was best to forget they had ever met.

He travelled home and threw himself into work at the peat bog, but it proved a poor distraction. If Sicily wasn't haunting his waking hours, she was there in his dreams. She inspired a confusing mass of contradictions—irritating but alluring, cruel but kind, threatening yet vulnerable. Tallow knew one thing for certain. He had to see her again. That conviction had him envisaging their next meeting.

A shape hurtled through the entrance to his cave, interrupting his reverie. A noisy eight-year-old bundle of energy bounced off the walls with laughter as he evaded Tallow's clutches.

"What's this?" The little troublemaker snatched up one of the sketches.

"Give that back, Screech." Tallow grabbed for the sketch, only provoking Screech further as the stakes of the game increased. Screech pulled on his tether and fled from the cave with his prize in hand.

"How many times do I have to tell you, Screech? Stay—out—of—my —cave!" Tallow yelled. He chuckled to himself, but sooner or later someone would need to discipline the boy.

Tallow returned to his drawing. He wasn't going to rise to the bait on his day off and spend the rest of the afternoon chasing Screech around the woods. Sooner or later, the boy would realize he was being ignored and find someone else to bother.

A pleasant and agreeably quiet hour passed before another shadow filled the cave entrance.

"I told you, Screech, stay out—oh, hi, Flint."

"What's the meaning of this?" The primelink demanded.

"I don't get a hello, Tallow, how are you today?"

Flint scowled. The man appeared grumpier than usual and Tallow decided not to provoke him further. "What have I done wrong now?" Tallow sighed.

"This!" Flint bellowed, holding out the sketch Screech had stolen.

Thanks a lot, Screech. Never was a name more aptly given.

"It's a sketch, Flint. You've seen them before. Why is your tether all tied up in knots?"

"It's a sketch of a woman!"

Tallow stood, annoyed by Flint's attitude. "I know, I drew it. So what? You can find drawings of females scattered throughout camp. You've shown me several yourself."

Flint's glare was full of accusation. "Those are crude scribbles, nothing like you're capable of drawing."

Tallow threw his arms up in exasperation. It seemed like no matter what he did, Flint would find something to complain about. "Let me get this straight. You're upset with me because I can draw better than others in the tribe?"

"No, you idiot! It's not the what, it's the how. Everyone admires the realism of your portraits, but they're just that, portraits. You draw from what you've seen and I want to know where you saw this woman!"

"I'm the tribe scout, Flint. I see lots of things in my travels. Why are you so upset?"

"I'm upset because you're undermining my authority."

"This again? How many times do I need to tell you? I don't want to be the primelink. I never did. You were my best friend, Flint. I was happy for you when you got the position."

Flint was shaking his head. "I barely won that vote. It could easily have been your hand holding the staff. Do you think I don't hear the murmurs when people disagree with my decisions? 'Tallow would never have done that,' they say. It's bad enough I have to compete with people's opinions of you without you feeding their romantic notions about a perfect leader."

"What are you talking about? I've always obeyed your every command and supported all of your decisions."

"Do you think I'm stupid, Tallow? Do you think I haven't noticed that every time a council takes place, the tribe watches to see how you'll vote before raising their own hands? You continually turn the people against me, and now this!"

"For the last time, Flint, I don't want your job. No conspiracy exists. How could it? You send me out on one scouting mission after another. Some might think you were hoping I'd meet with a terrible accident. Even so, I never complain. When I'm in the camp, I keep to myself as much as possible which is what I was doing when Screech invaded my isolation—and now you. I can hardly keep out of your way more than I do now."

"I notice you still haven't answered my question."

Tallow rolled his eyes. "Yes, I saw a woman, what difference does it make?"

Flint was seething as he ground out the words. "The difference, Tallow, is that the primelink is the first to receive a wife among the eligible men during his reign. Screech showed that sketch to just about everyone in the camp before he brought it to me. The tribe knows you drew it and now they're wondering how it is that you've seen a woman before the primelink has. They're wondering if you've received favour from the Luminaries and have a wife hidden somewhere. They wonder if a change in leadership is coming."

"That's ridiculous! It was a Tellusan woman on the other side of the limen. I couldn't have a relationship with her, even if I wanted to. Surely you knew I might spot a Tellusan at some point in my travels. It was purely coincidental that it happened to be a woman."

"Why did you keep that from me?"

"I didn't think it was important! Tellusans are just as afraid to cross the limen as we are. They don't cross to our side and we don't cross to theirs. I saw no threat to warn you about. The sighting had no bearing on my mission. I'm looking for resources when I'm out there, not people."

"You're a *scout*, Tallow! Reporting what you see is the very definition of your role. I'll decide if the information you give me is of importance—not you. As the primelink, I have standing orders to report any Tellusan activity near the limen to the Vigil."

"Well, how was I supposed to know that?"

Flint let out a groan of exasperation. "You *aren't* supposed to know about that, Tallow. You're supposed to report everything you see and leave it with me. You still haven't told me where you saw the woman."

"I don't know precisely. It was at least a two-week journey from here.

I would recognize my markers if I came across them again, but I didn't bother to map specific coordinates."

"Isn't that convenient? Almost as convenient as Screech passing this sketch around to start some rumours. How do the Tellusans fit into your plan?"

"There—is—no—plan. I'm not plotting against you. Whatever conspiracy you may be inventing is a figment of your imagination. Neither you nor the tribe is in any danger. Further, no one in this camp would believe that I have a secret wife who remains with me here in the swath. Never in our history has such a thing occurred. Even if it were so, what tribesman, given such a gift, would leave her to fend for herself in the swath for weeks at a time and miles away from any help? You're blowing this whole thing way out of proportion. I'll happily explain to the tribe that I stumbled across a Tellusan woman and made some sketches."

Flint squinted at Tallow, trying to spot a scheme. "You'll do no such thing."

"Fine! If my presence is so disruptive, I'll leave immediately for my next scouting trip." Tallow started shoving supplies into his pack.

"I'm afraid I can't allow that. You will remain in your cave until I give you permission to leave. I'll have Bull deliver food and water."

"What? You can't do that!"

"There you go again, assuming authority you have no claim to. Whether you like it or not, I'm the leader of the Blackspike Tether Tribe and I most certainly can order you detained. You will remain here until I've had a chance to speak with Vigil Strom on this matter. He will inform me of any concerns the Luminaries may have about the Tellusans you've seen. I'll decide what to tell the rest of the tribe about your drawing."

"It could be weeks before Vigil Strom returns." Tallow protested. "I need to get back out there and find another peat bog. We can't afford the delay."

"You're not going anywhere until I have the blessing of the Luminaries. Far more is at stake here than you realize."

Flint walked toward the mouth of the cave, blocking out the sunlight. He turned his head to speak over his shoulder in a voice as menacing as the shadow he cast. "If you disobey my orders, Tallow, I'll have you suspended from a tether. You've gone too far this time and I'm not going to put up with it anymore."

Tallow watched Flint storm off toward his own cave. He'd never seen the primelink so agitated. It didn't make sense. Since when did the tribe worry about the affairs of the Luminaries, other than for the exchange of goods? The tribes remained isolated and apart from the rest of the world, unaware and unconcerned with the broader political landscape. What could possibly be so important about his sighting of a lone Tellusan in this remote part of the world? Why would Flint be waiting for the Vigil's permission to do anything? What did he mean when he said, "far more is at stake than you realize?"

Sicily's question came back to haunt him. "What does it feel like to be a slave to the Luminaries?" He'd told her that the tether tribes were slaves to no one. Suddenly he wasn't so sure. What did the primelink know? What secrets were Flint and Vigil Strom keeping from the rest of the tribe? Was Sicily correct about the other things she'd said? He needed to talk to her again.

Sicily! He wouldn't be able to get back in time for the deadline he'd set. She'd think he never wanted to see her again. Tallow felt ill. He stood and walked to the entrance of the cave only to find Bull posted as a guard. Apparently, Flint wasn't taking any chances. There seemed little likelihood of leaving before the Vigil's return, but Tallow swore he'd find a way to see Sicily again.

6

Vigil Eli Strom stepped off the sky lift platform and clipped his harness to the ground tether that led toward the encampment. It was a necessary security measure to position the lift in an area clear of trees, usually in the desert of the interior beyond the treeline that hugged the limen. Decades ago, a few tribesmen had tried to climb the lift to get to their wives. Since then, it was protocol to create a separation between the lift and the camps. None of the tribesmen would leave the safety of the trees to risk freerise. The only way to the lift was by the ground tether which was always reeled in when the Vigil left.

Eli hated using tethers. He'd never learned how to traverse them with any kind of finesse. It made him feel clumsy and incompetent. He understood that the grace displayed by the tether tribes came from a lifetime of practice, but it annoyed him that someone inferior to him in status could be better than him at anything. Once again, he found himself dragging his flailing body hand over hand in sight of everyone. It was utterly humiliating. Of course, that was the point of this posting. The Luminaries only assigned tether tribe duty to those they wished to discipline. It was literally as low as you could go in the command hierarchy.

Eli reflected on the circumstances that brought him here. He'd had the temerity to question the wisdom of a superior officer. The man gave an order that would have placed his men in a dangerous position. His protests fell on deaf ears and several members of his squad died in the poorly planned operation. That same officer blamed Eli for their deaths. Concern for his subordinates had almost cost Eli his career. Lesson learned—since then, he only looked out for himself.

Strom's eyes followed the lift chain into the sky. It was going to be a long slow climb back into the good graces of the Luminaries. All the more reason to make sure his current assignment went without a hitch. He might only be the Vigil for the third sector of the southern limen, but he'd make himself look good in the process or die trying.

In an attempt to lessen the blow to his ego, Strom made it a habit to arrive when he knew most of the tribe was working the peat bog. He pulled himself the final three feet and breathed a sigh of relief as he left the desert environment and passed into the cool shade of the treeline. Eli reached for the boot clips tied to a tree and strapped them to his feet while he surveyed the encampment. The Blackspike Tether Tribe fastened bamboo ladder bridges between trees throughout the camp. Eli had to admit it was a practical solution to life at the bottom of the swath. Tethers were always necessary, but locking your feet onto the ladder rungs freed your arms for other tasks. As with the tethers, walking the ladder was an awkward process. Even so, Eli preferred it—the ladders provided a solid surface that made him feel more in control. It helped to know that he wasn't the only one who looked clumsy using it. The processes of locking and unlocking the clamps produced an unnatural gait that couldn't be avoided.

As he'd hoped, other than the primelink, and his right-hand man, Bull, the camp was practically empty. A few children were spinning at the ends of their tethers wrapping around a tree trunk, but they paid no attention to his arrival.

On closer inspection, he could see that Bull was arguing with someone in the mouth of a nearby cave. A face came briefly into view before the owner was shoved back into the cave. What was the scout doing here? He should have been out mapping the limen. Bull took up a guard position outside the cave entrance. That didn't bode well. Eli sighed. He'd been hoping for a quick, uneventful trip to the surface this time around. No such luck, Primelink Flint was already leaping toward him, calling out with a loud voice and drawing unwanted attention.

"Vigil Strom! Welcome! We've been eagerly awaiting your return."

Eli growled in frustration. He had zero respect for Flint, who was always blaming others for the tribe's shortcomings. The scout, in particular, was a common target of the primelink's rants for some imagined slight. Flint didn't seem to understand that respect was earned. "Can't this wait until we get to your cave? You know I'm not comfortable out here in the open."

Flint lowered his voice to a conspiratorial whisper. "Very wise, Vigil. Much of what we have to discuss is of a confidential nature."

Eli rolled his eyes. *Yet you fly through the camp bellowing at the top of your lungs.*

Flint's mouth was as open as the cave entrance the minute Eli stepped through.

"A woman, Vigil! Tallow saw a woman!" Flint thrust a sketch into Eli's hands. It was a very realistic rendering.

"He's plotting something, Vigil, I'm certain of it."

"Calm down, Flint. You know full well there are no women at the base of the swath. The only way down is via the sky lift, and it's not accessible by the public. I would know if a woman came to the surface. The Luminaries have no marriages scheduled for some time."

"That's just it, Vigil. The tribe has seen the sketch and thinks that the Luminaries have granted Tallow the first wife of this generation. That honour belongs to me!"

Eli rubbed his temples. He should have known it would be about wives. It was the singular focus of the tribes. How the Luminaries had managed to establish such a bizarre arrangement was beyond him. The *wives* were nothing more than ladies of the night and the tether tribe's *children*, denizens of the orphanage. Did the tribesmen really believe that their wedding night would always produce offspring? It didn't really matter, he supposed. The charade had the desired effect. It kept the tribes in line and future urchins off the streets.

"I assure you, Flint, that the Luminaries have not bestowed a wife on your scout. As I've said, no women have come down to the base of the swath."

Flint was shaking his head. "The woman was a Tellusan."

Eli straightened. "A. Tellusan woman was in the swath?"

"No, she was on the other side of the limen, but Tallow saw her and made that drawing. Now, my people are asking questions."

"When and where did this take place?"

"Over three weeks ago, Vigil."

"You're supposed to inform me when Tellusans are seen near the limen."

Flint was nodding vigorously, eager to explain. "Tallow was on a scouting mission and it took several days for him to return. He withheld that information from me until I discovered the sketch and confronted him. As you can see, we've kept Tallow under guard awaiting your arrival—which also took some time."

Eli grunted. True to form, Flint found a way to lay blame at everyone's feet, even the Vigil's.

"You've explained the delay. Were you planning to reveal the location?"

"I'm afraid I don't have the location. Tallow says he could find it again, not having marked the coordinates."

"Why not?"

"He didn't think it important. As he said, she was on the other side of the limen and posed no threat. I have to confess, Vigil, I also wonder why the Luminaries have made this request of the tether tribes. Why are you interested in the Tellusans?"

Good question, Eli thought. His own information was limited. All he knew was that a particular luminary had approached him in secret, requesting Eli deploy the tether tribes to keep an eye out for Tellusans near the limen. Eli was promised a reward for his vigilance and discretion. He knew only that a plan was in the works to move tether tribes into the interior of the swath, and that it was important the Tellusans remained in the dark.

Eli had devised a simple strategy to facilitate tether tribe relocation, hoping the luminary would recognize his initiative when it came time to receive his reward. All of the tether tribes under his purview were tasked with ongoing scouting missions for various resources. The Luminaries already had extensive maps showing the locations of the most valuable reserves. Telescope surveys conducted over the years had identified more than the scouts ever would. However, it was a good cover for the request. To reduce suspicion, it was important for the impetus to come from the tribes, themselves.

Eli found it worked well to incentivize a tribe by suggesting that a particular resource was in high demand. After that, it was a simple matter to chart promising caches found only deep within the interior and send the scouts out knowing they would eventually end up at the desired location. It wouldn't take much longer for the scouts to complete their exploration of the limen and turn their search to the interior. Eli hoped to have all of the tribes set up in new camps partway into the interior by the time the luminary came to him with the next phase of his plan.

Currently, Flint's tribe was the easiest to manipulate—partly because Flint wasn't that bright, but also because they already had an incentive as it became increasingly difficult to harvest peat in their current location. Eli had a new spot in mind along one of the tributaries. It was concerning that a Tellusan had been sighted. He needed to be certain that the woman hadn't been discovered near the chosen tributary. He couldn't afford to raise Tellusan suspicions. If he messed this up for the luminary, any further demotion would be of the permanent kind.

Eli considered what he could share with the primelink. It occurred to him that it didn't really matter what he said. Flint would believe anything the Vigil told him. All he needed was something imminently threatening, something beyond the tribe's ability to discover or understand. Isolated as they were, that wouldn't be difficult. The lie came easily and Flint absorbed his words with rapt attention, like a child before a storyteller.

"I shouldn't be telling you this." Eli began, "But the Tellusans are at war with the Luminaries. They seek to cripple us by cutting off the resources your people supply. Unfortunately, they've decided the most efficient way to accomplish this is by removing the workforce."

"Remove the workforce?" Flint interrupted, "What do you mean? Where would we go?"

"You wouldn't go anywhere, Flint. The tribe would be eliminated."

"They would kill us?" Flint shouted in alarm. "Why? The tether tribes have always kept to themselves. We remain apart from the politics of this world."

Eli shrugged in sympathy. "I had hoped it would never come to this. The Tellusans don't care about anyone but themselves. The Luminaries have always been friends to the tribes and we will try to protect you, but if a Tellusan has been spotted near the limen, it means they're searching for a target. You need to warn your people."

"I don't understand. The limen provides a bulwark. How would the Tellusans cross over?"

This is too easy, Eli thought. He wondered how fantastic a tale the man would believe and couldn't help himself. "The Tellusans have burrowing machines. They can pass beneath the limen and attack from below the surface. We have no way to know when or where they might strike."

Flint's eyes were wide with fear. "What should we do?"

"It may become necessary for the tribes to move away from the limen and travel inland. The burrowing machines have difficulty moving through the loose sands of the interior. It would afford the tribe some additional protection. I'll let you know if it comes to that, but I have another possible solution. Have your scout return to the place where he met this woman and release a buoy there. I can send the Luminary Navy to that location and rain death from the sky. That would effectively destroy any Tellusans in the area before they have an opportunity to harm you."

"You want me to release Tallow?" Flint sounded disappointed. "What if he's in league with the woman? Perhaps she crossed the limen in one of these burrowing machines and corrupted him."

Eli placed his palm across his eyes and let it slide down his face before taking a deep calming breath. "Does anyone else know the location of this Tellusan woman?"

"Only Tallow, Vigil."

"Then you really don't have a choice. Tell him what I've told you. You've expressed your concern about his ambition to replace you as primelink. Would he risk losing the tribe he wishes to lead? If it should turn out that he's a traitor to his people, we'll know soon enough. Right now, I need the location of these Tellusans."

Flint seemed uncertain, so Eli decided to throw him a bone. "I know the Luminaries would be grateful for your help in this matter. Under similar circumstances in the past, they've chosen to accelerate the marriage schedule to show their gratitude. Would that convince your people that you hold the favour of the Luminaries?"

Flint's eyes filled with a mixture of greed and desperate hope. "Yes, I can see how this would be the wisest course of action. The safety of the tribe must come first. I'll send Tallow at once."

Eli remained in the mouth of the primelink's cave long enough to watch the animated conversation between Flint and his scout. Eventually Tallow disappeared into the cave and returned with his gear. The scout turned his head to stare directly at Eli, before leaping to the trees.

Nothing remained for Eli to do until the scout returned, so he bumbled his way across the ladder bridges back to the treeline and the waiting tether. The desert sun was hotter than when he arrived and a groan escaped his lips as he began pulling his flailing body toward the sky lift. "I hate tethers!" he cursed. The tether responded by slamming him into a dune for a mouthful of sand. "And I hate sand!" Eli sputtered. By the time he reached the sky lift platform, his profanity had transformed into a prayer for a different posting.

7

On the final day of the third week, Sicily had remained at Tal's claw marked tree until the sun began to set. He hadn't shown up. The night that followed was a sleepless one and by the time the sun rose again she'd convinced herself that she must have mixed up the days. Did the tether tribes count their days from sunrise or sunset? Perhaps the delay was unavoidable. She continued to visit the tree daily, just in case. Today was the end of the fourth week and she had to admit to herself the two truths she'd been avoiding. First, Tal didn't want to see her again, she'd driven him off. Second, despite the fact she hardly knew him, she held strong feelings for him. The connection was undeniable. She felt empty inside and longed to see him again, even though her feelings made absolutely no sense. *Is this what my grandmother felt when she first saw my grandfather?*

Sicily had avoided scrutinizing the hopeful fantasy that Tal would cross the limen and help her leave Endelton for far-off lands filled with adventure. She knew she was delaying the inevitable, but accepting the truth meant closing and locking a door with the finality of a prison sentence. When reality threatened to invade and steal away her hope, she quickly replaced it with something equally pervasive—anger at her father for lying to her.

Her father had robbed her of a future and handed it all to Lomar. Sicily took pride in her ability to run the farm, managing their affairs on her own. It proved to be a fantasy every bit as idealized as a tether tribesman coming to her rescue. She wasn't even truly taking care of her father through her efforts. Everything belonged to Lomar. The eggs they ate, the milk she delivered for extra income, the vegetables from the garden, all courtesy of Lomar who was secretly supporting the indigent of Endelton. She would never have guessed the Basurto family would be among them. All along, she'd been a charity case unable to reclaim what was lost. How many knew about their situation? For years, people had listened to her vow that she'd make it on her own and travel the world. How must that have sounded to others acquainted with the truth? The very thought filled Sicily with mortification. Was that the reason Alisha told her to grow up? *Oh, please no.*

Did she have it all wrong? Was Alisha patient? Was Lomar good?

It wasn't fair. Her father had placed her in Lomar's debt without her knowledge. She surely owed Lomar her gratitude, but it was a debt she would never have accepted for herself.

Please come back to me, Tal. How can I stay here now? The shame is unbearable.

She'd decided that today would be the last day she would check the tree. She had to make a decision. As she walked to the meeting place, her time was spent in an agonizing examination of the few options left to her.

She could ask the tinker to escort her to the next town, but what then? She didn't have enough money to start a new life. If she could get an escort to the nearest monastery, she could seek sanctuary, but she'd still require a mount to carry her. Lomar had many. *And what about Papa?* Lomar could cancel her father's debt.

Maybe she should marry Lomar and save up money. Then, one day while on a trip abroad, she could run away. It wasn't a great solution, but it would ensure the forgiveness of her father's debt before she left. Unfortunately, the first trip Lomar had planned was scheduled for two years from now. That wouldn't work. Lomar had decided to have a family, and no doubt he planned to start immediately. She could be pregnant long before they ever left Endelton. Once children were involved, she could never leave, nor would she want to.

What other options did she have? As Lomar had pointed out, most of the other eligible bachelors were not much better off than she was. They could probably provide for her, but certainly not her father. That future held zero options for escape.

The Marin brothers had their winery. She had plenty of transferable skills she could offer. It might not make her much money and she'd still be stuck in Endelton, but at least she could regain some self-respect and she'd have interesting work to set her mind to. She could also help out her father a little. Sadly, it was true that the brothers liked to imbibe a little too much. She wasn't sure what that would look like in a marriage context. She'd never been around them when they were deep in their cups. What if they turned into mean drunks some day? She'd heard of it happening to others. That might be worse than Lomar.

Ugh—it always comes back to Lomar. Could Papa be right? Has he changed? Sicily shook her head. No, his assessment of her male friends had been condescending and mean-spirited. She knew in her heart that Lomar was still cruel, even if he had matured. The question was, how would it manifest and could she afford to take the chance? A harsh laugh escaped her lips. *Afford to? How can I afford otherwise?*

Sicily knew Lomar was the only practical solution to her problems. Maybe it wouldn't even be as bad as she was imagining. Lomar was far from the man of her dreams, but he wasn't hard to look at. Everyone kept telling her that people can fall in love with just about anyone, eventually. These types of marriages were common in small remote communities. The problem was, the whole affair felt like manipulation and she didn't think she could ever get past that to see Lomar in a different light.

Sicily stopped just short of the limen, facing the tree on the other side. Her insides twisted with anxiety. She didn't want to think of Lomar anymore, but neither did she wish to lift her gaze and face the rejection of Tal. She did her best to prepare herself for the inevitable. *This is it, Sicily. You can't keep coming here. Time to make a decision.*

She lifted her eyes to the three marks, but saw six instead.

She shook her head and squinted, but the lines remained. *He'd been here!* She couldn't believe it. When had he come? She should have stayed a little longer yesterday. Was she too late? The thought had her trembling. It was too much. She couldn't take one more disappointment.

"Sicily." His voice came from higher up in the tree.

She shivered at the sound of her name. Her heart began to race. Tears came, unbidden. She didn't lift her head. Falling to her knees instead, she wrapped her arms around her body trying to hold herself in the moment. "I'm so sorry, Tal! Forgive me. I made a mistake. Please stay. I know it's crazy, but I—I need you."

Tallow changed position so he was at the same level. "It's okay, Sicily. There's nothing to forgive. I feel the same."

"When you failed to return, I thought you never wanted to see me again."

"I know, I'm sorry, Sicily. I had every intention of returning, but Primelink Flint placed me under guard. I felt sick wondering what you must be thinking. After all this time, I didn't expect to find you here, but I had to try."

"You're not angry anymore about the things I said?" Sicily rose and looked into his eyes, finding forgiveness there, and maybe something more.

"No, I think you may be right. I'm still not sure about the murder of senior tribesmen, but *something* strange is going on. The primelink was furious when he found out I'd seen a Tellusan. He said he was under standing *orders* to report any Tellusan activity near the limen. He was following the orders of the Vigil. It's as you said...." Tallow looked away. "It appears that we serve the Luminaries.

"I remained in confinement until the Vigil returned. He said that the

Luminaries are at war with the Tellusans. He said your people are planning to attack the tether tribes. He claimed that you want to exterminate us. It makes no sense. The tether tribes have nothing to do with external politics."

Sicily laughed. "Attack the tether tribes? Tal, our village consists of farmers and artisans. As far as I know, we're not at war with the Aerish. Even if we were, no one from Endelton would pass as a warrior. Besides, how would we cross the limen?"

"The Vigil said that the Tellusans have burrowing machines that can pass under the limen and attack from below."

"That sounds a bit far-fetched to me, but the tinker might have some answers. He could certainly tell us if a war had erupted. He's in the village for the next few weeks. Would you be willing to meet with him? I could bring him tomorrow morning."

"Yes, I would like to hear from him myself."

"As for the other things I told you, I owe you an explanation. Will you let me show you something? It's about a quarter mile east of here."

"I came for answers. Can I see it from this side of the limen?"

Sicily nodded. "It's a large stone resting as close to the limen as you can get. It's impossible to miss. You can travel faster than I can, why don't you go on ahead and I'll catch up? I think you may want to see it for yourself before I offer explanations."

Tallow looked as if he wanted to say more. Instead, he shrugged and headed east.

It took Sicily twenty minutes to wind her way through the trees. When she arrived at the stone, Tallow had obviously seen it and looked to be deep in thought. He hadn't noticed her arrival, so she watched him silently for a moment, trying to get a read on his reaction.

"What do you think?"

Tallow looked at her with pursed lips, then turned toward the rock and began to read the words that had been inscribed on a polished surface facing the swath.

"To my brothers of the tether tribes, I leave this stone as witness. The Luminaries have lied to us. I saw them cut the tethers of our elders. No future remains for us under their control, only death. I tried to tell our primelink, but he didn't believe me. I chose to leave rather than face that same end. I have crossed the limen and settled in the land of the Tellusans. What we have been told about the dangers of crossing are also lies. I not only survived, but built a home and a life. My wife, Elsa, has given me a daughter. My daughter, Shale, gave birth to my beautiful granddaughter, Sicily. My life has been a full and happy one. If you're reading this, I beg you to consider the crossing before it is too late. Tell others about this place and encourage them likewise."

Sicily waited for the inevitable question.

"Is Sicily a common name, or is this man your grandfather?"

"My grandfather, yes."

"This is how you know so much about the tether tribes."

Sicily nodded, but held her tongue.

"The stone is signed by Trapper of the Blackspike Tether Tribe. I know of this man. He trained the scout who mentored me in turn. My generation tells the story of Trapper's disappearance as a lesson about the dangers of carelessness. Trapper left on a scouting mission one day and never returned. The tribe assumed he had fallen into the ether."

"Do you believe the message is genuine?"

"Without a doubt. Do you see that piton embedded into the top of the stone? The design and colour are unique to the Blackspike Tribe. No one else would have such a thing in their possession and know where it came from."

"Will you consider it?"

"Telling other tribesmen about this place and the danger to their lives? Of course."

Sicily looked at her feet. "I meant, will you consider the crossing? My grandfather planted this tree beside the stone decades ago. As you can see, its branches straddle the limen. He meant for it to serve as a bridge to ease the passage.”

Tallow took a step closer and lifted his hand to reach out to Sicily, then let it fall back to his side. “I very much want the life your grandfather describes. I’d like to find out if that life will include you, but I can’t turn my back on my brothers. Before I consider crossing, I need to attempt to convince them of the truth. To do that I need more information, information I’m hoping your tinker can provide.”

Sicily nodded, having guessed he would answer as he did. It wasn’t really a surprise that Tal thought of others before himself. She had sensed that about him. It drove away any doubts she may have had about misjudging Lomar who thought first of himself. Lomar might have outgrown much of the blatant cruelty he displayed as a child, but it lingered in some form, lacking the kind of integrity she observed in Tallow.

Sicily felt a burden lifting. She had her answer and it wasn’t Lomar. Tal hadn’t made any promises, but he was interested in seeing where a relationship might lead. She didn’t want to read more into it than that. Sicily was the first woman Tal had ever met. It was entirely possible that once he met others, he’d lose interest in her. Still, she was confident that he would help her trek through the wilderness to a new life in a different place. If they parted ways after that, it would break her heart, but at least she had the means for her escape, affording her a little optimism. It felt good to hope again. “I’ll return with Adis in the morning. We can talk more after that.”

“Thank you, Sicily.”

“For what?”

“For caring about what happens to me—and my people. You would make a fine brother in my tribe, except you’re far too pretty and I don’t need more brothers.”

Sicily smiled. “It would be an honour to be recognized as a sister of the Blackspike Tether Tribe. I’m a descendant, after all. I know my grandfather would relish the thought.”

"I don't think I want to call you Sis." Tallow grinned. "When tribesmen meet for the first time, we embrace in a bond of camaraderie. I look forward to that embrace with you."

Tallow's expression suggested much more than camaraderie and Sicily felt her face heating. "I look forward to that moment, too."

Sicily turned and started to walk back to the village, then stopped to look over her shoulder. "You'll still be here, right?"

"You have my word."

Those four words had a stronger emotional impact than she expected. At the moment, she didn't trust any of the other men in her life, but she *did* trust Tal. Sicily smiled and fell into a jog. She needed to find Adis and fill him in. Then she needed her bed. Her nights had been restless since she learned about her father's debt. Sicily's stomach growled, reminding her that she hadn't been eating much either. *I can eat tomorrow*, she decided. The promise of a peaceful sleep for the first time in weeks seemed more important. Her stomach protested. *Okay, a quick snack and then bed.* It was good to have options.

8

Adis and Sicily didn't arrive at the stone until late morning, delayed by the tinker's routine of selling last-minute supplies to the workmen before they headed out to the field. That was fine with Sicily. She'd rather the villagers not see her heading off with the tinker. He'd locked up his cart and slipped away to meet at her house. Well, Lomar's house she supposed. Tallow was waiting for them when they reached the limen. He was chewing on some sort of stringy dried meat. *I wonder what kind of meat that is. Game animals don't exist in the swath.* Some small mammals in a nearby tree drew her attention and she decided she'd rather not know.

Adis waved and called out to Tallow. "Hello, my young friend! Sicily has told me a great deal about you and I've been eager to meet you."

"I'm sorry, but I'm not sure I can say the same." Tallow replied honestly.

"Indeed, your circumstances are unfortunate, but I assure you our meeting is auspicious. At least, I hope that will prove to be the case."

"Sicily tells me you know something about the history of my people. May I ask how you came across your information?"

Adis smiled. "I understand your reluctance to take my word for things. Much about the tether tribes remains a mystery to those of us on this side of the limen. If the shoe were on the other foot, I would feel the same." Adis placed his hand on his chin and tapped the side of his nose as he considered the best approach. "I've spoken at great length with Sicily's grandfather before he died. I learned a little about your culture from his stories, and I've heard his testimony firsthand. But you've read the stone and talked with Sicily, so you already know all of this."

Tallow nodded for the tinker to continue.

"I assume Sicily explained that tinkers carry news from place to place. What she may not have mentioned is that tinkers function for a number of governments in an official capacity. We don't deal in rumours, we deal in official documentation. We're sanctioned to gather intelligence related to global interests. We're the eyes and ears for those who maintain international treaties. Sometimes that's the only thing that keeps us from war. In that capacity, I can already answer one of your questions. The Luminaries are not at war with the Tellusans. The Vigil lied to your primelink.

"Sicily also mentioned that you have some questions about crossing the limen. I've travelled through both the northern and southern limens and spent time in the Tropos Archipelago in the upper parts of the swath. I assure you that your bones won't collapse and your organs won't implode. The risk of a long fall is the only danger. In your case, the drop would be very short. The same is true at the upper limits of the swath where the direction of gravity returns to normal at twelve thousand feet. Embassies exist in the mountain ranges at that elevation where people routinely cross the limen in both directions. It's true that those who have spent their entire lives in half gravity experience sore muscles, but it's only a temporary discomfort—easily bearable."

"What of the burrowing machines?" Tallow asked.

Adis laughed. "If such a thing existed, I can tell you that the tinkers would be very interested in getting their hands on one. It would be useful in certain, say, clandestine endeavours. No such technology exists, I'm afraid. The Tinker's Guild is far-reaching. Something like that couldn't remain hidden from us."

"So the Vigil lied about that, too."

"Yes," Adis agreed. "The question remains as to his purpose for doing so. It might be helpful at this point if I gave you a little context." Adis looked pointedly at Sicily and seemed to come to a decision. "Come closer, Sicily. You're bound up in this, too. Your grandfather started something and you might as well know what you're getting into."

Sicily lifted a questioning eyebrow and drew near.

"Tallow, the information I can give you is less about tether tribe ways, and more about the history of your people as recorded in the official documentation of the governments that encompass you. When you add these details to what you already know, I think you'll find it very illuminating and you'll begin to share my concerns.

"Early on in the development of the floating cities that make up the Tropos Archipelago, crime was rampant. It was a wild new frontier, and people were fighting for a stake. At first, the founders tried a zero tolerance policy. The slightest infraction could earn a death sentence. That was a brief and brutal time, but it quickly became apparent that they couldn't continue to deplete their workforce. Instead, they decided to send criminals to the base of the swath. There they worked at harvesting what they could from the surface while chained to the same. It worked. No one wanted to spend the rest of their lives struggling against the pull at their chains. Most considered it a fate worse than death and crime plummeted as a result."

"Tallow and his brothers were raised in the swath. It's the only life they know. Are the Aerish convicting children now?" Sicily wondered.

"That's the crux of the problem. The founders had become dependent on the resources provided by that workforce. Unfortunately, workers aged and died and fewer criminals were available to replace them. At the same time, other governments began to protest and demanded an end to the chain gangs.

"In those days, both men and women were sent to the surface. It was inevitable that children would be born, pushing the founders to ensure this potential new workforce remained hidden from the public eye. They decided to raise the boys in isolation. Over time, they developed a culture, never having known anything else. Their captivity became their heritage based on a system of work for reward. Our records show a disturbing correlation between the disappearance of children from orphanages and the replacement of tether tribe members. I'm sure you've guessed by now that the tether tribes are the descendants of those convicts. Your people are the result of a criminal social experiment, an attempt to create an entire culture of willing servants."

Tallow paled. "You're suggesting that the practice is still occurring. How could it be that no one notices?"

"The founders told the world they had dismantled the camps. No Tellusan would risk freerise to check. As for the Aerish, the location of the sky lifts are a closely guarded secret. Very few would have access to the camps even if they wanted to visit the surface—which they don't. Time has passed, the atrocity forgotten within a single generation. As for the orphanages, they're filled with the offspring of people unwilling to take responsibility for their choices. Many of those are people in positions of authority who turn a blind eye."

Sicily's eyes were wide with shock. "That's horrible! Those poor children."

Tallow completed the thought. "And I am one of those children."

Sicily turned tear filled eyes in Tal's direction, wishing she could comfort him in some way.

"We don't know that for certain," Adis corrected. "That's our suspicion, but we have no way to prove it. The Tinker's Guild has been trying to expose this ongoing atrocity for decades, but we've never had any actionable intelligence. As you well know, Tallow, the tether tribes are very isolated and almost impossible to contact. Yet, here you are."

Tallow glanced at Sicily and then returned his attention to Adis. "You want my help," he realized.

"The Tinker's Guild has uncovered whispers of an Aerish plot to undermine the peace accord. We know very little, only that it involves something about to take place in the interior of the swath. If the Vigil is asking your headsman to monitor the limen, it suggests he has something to hide. It's not a lot to go on, but if we can show that the Luminaries are active at the base of the swath, it may raise enough concern to begin an investigation."

"And if an investigation takes place, the plight of the tether tribes will come to light." Sicily guessed.

"Exactly. As I said, it's not a lot to go on. We have no guarantee of a positive outcome, but this is the biggest lead we've had in a very long time."

"What is it you'd like from me?" Tallow asked.

"The same as Sicily's grandfather. I'd like you to warn others and bring them to the stone. I can have the Guild station someone here permanently to watch for tribesmen. It would allow free sharing of information in both directions." Adis reached into his satchel and pulled out a wrapped package. "I have some photographs of the stone and Trapper in his tether tribe garments, surrounded by his family. I also have documents containing the history of the chain gangs we've discussed. They might be useful in helping you persuade others."

Tallow moved in a slow spiral up, and down the tree he was clinging to. Sicily had come to recognize the action as his equivalent of pacing. After a minute or so, he descended. "This is a lot to process. I was already questioning the actions of my tribe's primelink before I spoke with you. After I read Trapper's message on the stone, I was prepared to warn my brothers based on that information alone. I'll gratefully accept whatever evidence you can provide to help me convince them to see for themselves, but there is something I should let you know."

"Please—any information could be important."

"I was ordered to place a buoy at this location so the Luminaries could send their navy. The Vigil said their vessels would send a rain of fire to protect the tether tribes from the imminent Tellusan threat. He said they could destroy the burrowing machines. Clearly, that wasn't the truth, but I was warned against speaking with Sicily again. If I don't send up this buoy, they will become suspicious. If that happens, I won't be of any use to you or my tribe."

Sicily gasped, placing her hand over her mouth. "They want to bomb Endelton? We have to warn the village!"

Adis placed a hand on Sicily's arm. "Not to worry, they don't know where the village is yet. The Luminaries are trying to keep this quiet. They won't indiscriminately bomb up and down the limen. They'll want some assurance that a localized strike will have a reasonable degree of success. That's why they want the buoy."

Tallow looked from Adis to Sicily and back again. "What's a bomb?"

Sicily struggled to explain. "It's a—well—imagine if the fire within your cook stove burst from its confines and rapidly expanded to engulf your entire camp, incinerating everything in its path. Then imagine hundreds of stoves igniting at the same time."

Tallow's eyes widened. "They possess such a destructive item?"

"We may not have burrowing machines," Adis sighed, "but worse things exist."

"Raining fire." Tallow whispered. "I thought the Vigil was speaking in metaphor. What do you suggest I do?"

"The halfway point between the next village east of here is a three-day journey by carriage. If you were to release the buoy there, it would provide a good margin for safety. I assume you can travel faster through the trees than I can by winding road. Give me two days after you arrive. That will allow enough time for me to set up my telescopes and cameras. I'll need to create a record of the attack when it happens—if it happens. This could be momentous, Tallow. If the Aerish Navy is brazen enough to send bombs across the limen providing me evidence of their plans, it will be a clear breach of the treaty and an investigation will ensue. It may be enough to demand access to the sky lifts."

The tinker found a stick and sketched a crude map on the ground. "This is the first river you'll cross moving east from here. It's close to the halfway point I mentioned. Once across the river, move to the treeline at the edge of the desert and look eastward into the swath." Adis placed a rock on the ground northeast of the undulating line representing a river. "You'll see a conspicuous butte. Line up with that and release the buoy."

Tallow nodded. "I can do that, but I won't have time to return here. Primelink Flint will expect me back by then. I will be cutting things close. I might be able to explain a day's delay, but no more."

"Then you'd better move quickly." Adis noted the position of the sun. "You still have a good eight hours of sunlight left. Good luck, Tallow, I'll be telling the Guild about you. If you should happen to cross the limen and find yourself in need of assistance, find a tinker. They'll be prepared to help."

Tallow began to apologize to Sicily, but she cut him off. "It's okay, Tal. I know you'll return after you do what needs to be done. Bring your brothers here. I'll be waiting."

9

Tallow found the location easily enough. From his vantage within the swath, he looked down into a valley surrounded by rocky bluffs. The vegetation in the area was scruffy due to the rocky soil. He could see why the tinker had suggested this spot. The topography would help to contain a fire and minimize damage to the surrounding forest. On further consideration, he supposed the tinker would also be able to capture images of the entire valley from a carefully selected point on one of the ridges.

Tallow wondered at the type of world the tinker lived in. One where every move required careful forethought. Marvels were there to discover, yes, but it seemed to Tallow that the Tellusans were also slaves of a sort. Could any of them leave their homes without advanced planning? Could they experience the joy of sailing between trees with nothing to consider other than the exhilaration of exploration? Up until this point in his life, the biggest danger he'd had to face was the risk associated with freerise—a consequence of his own choices. This new danger arose from the interference of others. Tallow grunted at his own naiveté for believing an illusion. The Luminaries had been manipulating him his entire life. He'd just been ignorant of the truth. His jailers had robbed him of his life as a child, too young to understand. Now that he did understand, they'd taken away any joy from his current life as well. Tallow felt an anger threatening to overtake him, but pushed it down. It would serve no good purpose at present.

It had taken him a day and a half to travel to the valley, so he only needed to wait for another half day before releasing the buoy. Tallow hoped that the tinker was able to get all of his equipment set up before the Luminary Navy made a move. He had never heard of a bomb before, but Sicily's description had been horrifying enough. He had no idea how large an area would be affected and worried about the tinker remaining behind as a witness. Tallow had considered delaying his return trip for a few days to see for himself. In the end, he decided he didn't really want destruction of that magnitude to haunt his dreams. Besides, he needed to get back before Flint became suspicious. It was going to be hard enough trying to convince him of the danger to the tribe without putting the primelink on edge beforehand.

The remaining hours passed quickly, and then it was time to leave. He'd completed the task demanded of him. The Luminary Navy would be moving along the limen searching for the buoy. When they located it, they would do whatever it was they were going to do and he wanted to be far away when it happened.

***

Tallow made good time as he travelled back toward the river he'd crossed on his way to the valley. He hardly noticed the hours go by, consumed with thoughts of the future—thoughts of Sicily. He had promised he would come back, but made no promises about what he would do once he returned. He knew she wanted him to cross the limen, and he wanted to be with her, to see where that relationship would lead. At the same time, he was terrified of plunging into a world he knew nothing about.

What would Sicily require of him? Could he fulfill her expectations, or would she be disappointed and leave him? Tallow was used to being alone, but abandoned in a strange land? The thought was distressing. He literally knew nothing of day-to-day life outside the swath. How would he provide for himself? What skills did a tether tribesman possess that were applicable on the other side of the limen? He might have nothing more to offer than the strength of his arms. Tallow shook his head at the mental picture of a tribesman labouring alongside a Tellusan. His output would be half that of others, due to the presence of full gravity. He would be weaker, unable to safeguard against dangers he knew nothing about. How would he effectively defend Sicily if he wasn't sure he could protect himself? From what Adis had told him, tensions existed between the Luminaries and the Tellusans. Would Tellusans accept Tallow, or would his half-gravity features mark him as an Aerish enemy in their eyes? How would he navigate the culture and the politics without making a fool of himself?

Tallow had almost convinced himself it would be better to flee into the interior of the swath and live out his life as a hermit, when the unexpected happened. He nearly collided with a scout from a different tether tribe, a rare and very welcome event. After the customary embrace and exchange of names, Tallow learned that his new acquaintance came from an encampment a few miles inland along the river he'd recently crossed. Whip was a member of the Fleetwood Tether Tribe. He and his brothers panned for gold along the riverbanks.

"You must come back to the camp with me," Whip insisted. "The tribe would welcome an exchange of stories."

"I would enjoy that very much, Whip, but I carry important information for my primelink. He's expecting me and I have little time."

"I can see that you've been travelling hard. You're running out of daylight, and you'll need to stop soon for the night. Surely our hospitality will offer better food and rest. It will strengthen you for the long day of travel ahead of you. The camp is close. You won't be going far out of your way. If you're concerned about interrupting our daily routine, don't be. We've finished our work for the day, and the Vigil has already left."

At the mention of the Vigil, a new worry consumed Tallow. He had placed a buoy not far from the Fleetwood Tribe. If the Luminaries were concerned about Tellusans wandering near the limen, what would they do if they thought Tellusans were close to a tether tribe settlement? What would that mean for the tribe? He may have inadvertently affected their future. It suddenly seemed very important to make sure the Fleetwood Tribe understood the truth about their lives. Tallow realized he didn't really have a choice. "You're right, my friend. I am tired from my travels and your hospitality would be welcome, but I believe I also need to warn your primelink about a danger to the tether tribes."

Whip's friendly demeanour turned solemn. "Then let us leave immediately."

As Whip had promised, they arrived in less than an hour with Whip immediately directing Tallow to the primelink. Several tribesmen watched with curious gazes as Tallow passed through their settlement. It was similar in some ways to his own, but he didn't notice any caves in the area. Instead, the Fleetwood Tribe had woven large orb-like baskets made of reeds from the riverbanks. Each was large enough for a man to sleep in, with room for their belongings. The nests hung like beads on a leather cord, strung together between the trees in a large circle. A much larger habitat hung in the centre. Hand-holds on the exterior provided a similar function to the ladder bridges he was familiar with. Tallow watched closely as Whip alternately reached for handholds or hooked his feet through loops. Soon Tallow was moving along just as swiftly as his guide. They were heading for the large sphere which Tallow assumed must be the residence of the primelink.

Whip paused at the entrance to announce their arrival. "Primelink Longshadow, I've returned with a guest."

The pod swayed with movement, and a head appeared in the opening. "What a welcome surprise! Who am I addressing?"

"My name is Tallow. I'm a member of the Blackspike Tether Tribe, located some distance west of you."

"Ah yes, the Blackspike Tribe. It has been many years since our two people have had contact. Please, make my home your own." The primelink motioned for Tallow to enter. "Whip, find a pod and food for our guest."

Whip left on his errand while Tallow and Primelink Longshadow shared the traditional embrace.

"Please, have a seat. Tell me, Tallow, what brings you to our camp?"

"I wish I could say it was just to rest on my journey and share stories, but I'm on an urgent mission. When I encountered Whip and learned of a tribe nearby, I thought it best to bring my warning to you as well. I'll need to leave at first light to bring this information back to my own tribe."

Primelink Longshadow frowned. "You look as though you have quite a tale to tell and an eagerness to share it quickly. I will hear it first before it comes to the ears of my people. Please, proceed."

Tallow hadn't considered how he would present his news. He decided to begin with information a little closer to home. "It begins with a man named Trapper from my own tribe, a scout who disappeared two generations ago."

The primelink's eyebrows rose. "I've heard this story as a child, a warning about the dangers of freerise. The Trapper who evaded his own snare, only to fly into the heavens."

Tallow smiled at the embellishment. "I'm surprised the tale has travelled so far."

Longshadow shrugged. "It's a convenient teaching aid. Such things take on a life of their own."

"Yes, well, it's more than a tale and I've recently learned that Trapper didn't die. He married, raised a daughter, and lived to see his granddaughter."

"You are stringing me along," Longshadow laughed. "It's a tall tale after all. I'll be curious to hear the reason for faking one's death on the verge of the hoisting. It's a curious spin on a popular theme."

"Trapper didn't accept the hoisting. He fled across the limen where he met his wife among the Tellusans."

"Now, that's an interesting twist I didn't see coming."

Tallow lifted his voice in frustration. "You're not hearing me. This isn't a story to tell around the cook stove. What I'm trying to tell you is that the hoisting is a deception. The Luminaries are killing elders. They've been lying to us!"

"You're serious."

Tallow nodded.

"Young man, I don't know how you do things in your tribe, but here, the primelink is respected. When my scout approaches me, he gives me facts, not games and riddles. I'm willing to accept that your ways may be different, but these are serious allegations that bring into question the very fabric of our society. I need to know right now if these are theatrics or if you believe your words to be truth. If it's the former, I'll need to ask you to leave. If the latter, you'd better have proof or you'll be escorted out of the camp in a very unpleasant manner."

"Have you ever seen elders board the sky lift?"

Longshadow thought for a moment. "No. We usually have the hoisting ceremony before the men leave the camp to work for the day. We don't see them again after we say our goodbyes."

"It's the same for the Blackspike Tribe."

Longshadow was shaking his head. "That doesn't mean elders are murdered."

"Trapper left for a mission following a hoisting ceremony. He forgot his grapple and returned to fetch it. The camp was empty and he saw the elders leaving for their reward. He thought he'd secretly watch their ascent. Instead he saw a Vigil cut their tethers. Trapper was nearing the time for his own hoisting and he didn't want to suffer the same fate, so he fled across the limen."

"What proof do you have? How would you even learn such a thing if Trapper left the swath?"

"Trapper left a stone of witness at the edge of the limen facing the swath. I have seen it myself." Tallow handed the primelink one of the Blackspike Tribe's distinctive spiral pitons. "One of these pitons is embedded in the stone of witness. It didn't cross the limen on its own and engrave a message. I have also spoken with Trapper's granddaughter who confirmed the matter. If that were not enough, she brought a tinker to the limen. He's like a keeper of the histories for the Tellusans and the Luminaries. He explained to me the origin of the tether tribes, along with convincing proof."

Tallow dug through his pack and pulled out the package provided by Adis. He carefully unwrapped the glass-encased photographs and handed them to Longshadow. "The Tellusans have devices that can extract perfect drawings of the world. The tinker called these drawings photographs. These images show the stone of witness and Trapper with his family. The young woman on the right is the person I spoke with."

"This is remarkable! The images are so lifelike." Longshadow looked up from the photographs as a new thought entered his mind. "You've seen a woman."

"Anyone can see a woman at any time, on the other side of the limen."

"Truly?"

"I've created a detailed map with landmarks. You can visit the stone and see for yourself. If you remain for a time, you can speak with Trapper's granddaughter. She has agreed to check for visitors from time to time."

Tallow shared the rest of the documents outlining tether tribe history. By the time he reached the end of his narrative, Longshadow was nearly bursting with anger.

Tallow was relieved that Longshadow was taking him seriously. "The tinker has asked me to encourage any tribesman I meet to visit the stone and consider crossing the limen. He says the Luminaries are planning something that could harm the tether tribes. I need to warn you that the Luminaries are planning to rain fire across the limen, not far east of here.

You should avoid that area for the time being. If you see smoke in the sky in days to come, you can travel there and witness Luminary treachery for yourselves."

"How do you know about this?

"Because, under the command of Vigil Strom, Primelink Flint ordered me to release a buoy there as a marker for that purpose. The Luminaries want to destroy Tellusans who they believe will be at that location."

"Strom? Is he your Vigil as well? And your primelink took orders from him? This is unacceptable! Several weeks ago Vigil Strom told me to send a scout along the limen and report any Tellusans spotted nearby. I told him that the tether tribes have nothing to do with external politics—that we wouldn't be wasting time on such endeavours. He threatened to withhold our brides if I didn't comply. Can you imagine? Denying us our birthright as though he could ignore the credit we've invested. I laughed in his face, but after all you've told me, I wonder if those were idle threats."

"Vigil Strom has been lying to all of us." Tallow agreed. "The Luminaries threaten our way of life—not just the life we know, but the life they stole from us in the first place."

Longshadow played with the string of gold beads around his neck. "I recognize firsthand that something has changed in how the Vigil is treating us, and I'm inclined to believe what you've told me. However, it falls to me to determine the truth of a matter before I act. These photographs from your tinker are compelling, but I wish to set living eyes on the stone, itself. I know you've seen it, but I'd like additional confirmation from a member of my own tribe. I will send Whip to the stone and if we see smoke to the east, I will send him to investigate that as well. If my scout can verify what you've told me, I'll be confronting the Vigil."

"That is wise, Primelink. I'll be travelling past the stone on my way back. I would be happy to guide Whip there myself if he's free of other duties."

"What could be more pressing than learning the truth? I'll have Whip gather provisions and accompany you in the morning. As for now, you need to eat and rest. I am sure this day has already lasted longer than you'd planned."

"Thank you, Primelink."

"Perhaps when we've resolved this matter, you can return here so I can give you a proper Fleetwood welcome."

"I'd like that." Tallow smiled. "I wish you a good night, Primelink."

10

Tallow arrived back home at the end of the workday. The tribe had begun to gather around the tethered cook stove to prepare the evening meal. Sicily's description of a bomb sprang to mind and he shuddered at the mental picture of flames engulfing the camp and his brothers. The tribe had never felt threatened by the Luminaries, but the knowledge he now carried about their duplicity and power made him very uncomfortable. What would the Luminaries do if the tribe opposed them? What if the Luminaries simply grew tired of the tether tribes? How could his tribe hope to defend itself? The only weapon they had was foreknowledge. They could escape into the trees and live without luminary interference if they chose to, but would they? Would his tribe willingly give up the life they knew and the opportunity for a bride?

Tallow was greeted warmly as he joined his brothers in the evening meal preparations. He decided to wait for the entire tribe to gather before sharing his news. The primelink was always last to arrive, not partaking in the preparations himself. It wasn't a traditional privilege, Flint just didn't enjoy the task. It was one of the many reasons Flint had never earned the admiration he coveted from his tribe. Tallow tried to explain it to him once, but Flint was so convinced that Tallow was the source of his problems that it fell on deaf ears.

The air filled with pleasant conversation and the delicious aroma of rodent stew. Tallow's stomach rumbled in anticipation. He'd endured weeks of travel rations. *I should probably say something before Flint shows up and places me in confinement again.*

"Everyone, I have important news to share."

"Can't this wait until after we've eaten?"

"Go ahead and fill your bowls, but please give me your ears as you do so."

The group grunted their agreement and lined up for a turn at the stew pot. Tallow dove into the narrative he'd given the primelink of the Fleetwood Tribe.

"I recently discovered that Trapper, our former scout, didn't die as we thought." Laughter arose from the group, but Tallow pushed on. "He crossed the limen and took a wife from among the Tellusans." Several scoffed and Tallow noticed Bull slipping away, no doubt to get Flint.

"It's true. He left a stone with a graven message, bearing witness. I can take you there, so you can see it for yourselves."

Flint arrived with a scowl on his face, pointing a finger at Tallow. "You have no authority to convene a council."

Tallow rolled his eyes. "This isn't a council, Flint. I'm merely sharing the story of my journey with the tribe, as is customary when we gather around the camp stove."

"I warned you before, Tallow, I am the primelink and you're to report what you see to me."

"Or what?" Tallow shot back. "You'll confine me to my cave again? When has a primelink ever done such a thing? Why are you upset? Is it because I share with the tribe as scouts have always done? Are you trying to hide something?"

The tribe shared uncomfortable glances. Very rarely did a tribesman challenge their leader so openly. They waited for an answer to the accusation.

Flint surveyed the questioning faces, turning to address the group. "You elected me as your primelink, however Tallow has been questioning my authority ever since. By doing so, he suggests that your vote carries no worth. Now he defies me openly, calling me by name instead of using my title. Do you doubt he seeks the staff of leadership for himself? Have you ever heard of such a thing? Do you wonder then why he was confined? Unprecedented provocations require an unprecedented response."

"I have never sought the staff of leadership." Tallow responded. "That wasn't the reason I was confined to my cave. It was because the primelink forbade me from sharing information with the rest of you—information you have every right to hear."

"It's Tallow who is withholding information. Did none of you wonder that he had such a detailed drawing of a woman? I know you've been asking yourselves whether Tallow has a secret wife."

Heads were nodding as Tallow raised his hands and his voice to quiet the growing murmurs. "I would have happily explained the drawings to the rest of you. I offered to do that very thing, but again, the primelink forbade it. You know what followed. I had no opportunity to speak to any of you, and afterwards I was quickly dispatched on a mission for the Vigil." That revelation stunned the tribe. The Vigil did not have authority to dictate commands to the tribe.

"I will explain the drawings to you now, assuming the primelink doesn't forbid your right to hear it."

Flint glowered at Tallow, his countenance filled with warning.

"I don't have a wife, but I did meet a Tellusan woman who spoke to me from the other side of the limen. She's the woman depicted in my drawings."

The murmurs started again as Tallow continued. "I met this woman at the stone of witness of which I spoke. She's Trapper's granddaughter. I can take you to meet her. She will verify the truth written on the stone."

The murmurs grew to shouts, demanding answers.

"He's lying to you!" Flint shouted. "See how little he respects your intelligence? Bull tells me that Tallow has made claims that Trapper lived and took a Tellusan wife. Now we're to believe he has spoken to the man's granddaughter? We all know that no one can cross the limen and survive. Why would Trapper, a man who was close to the hoisting, risk his reward by attempting to cross the limen? I didn't share this with the tribe because it sounded too ridiculous—too unbelievable. I thought perhaps Tallow had eaten some vision berries. I sent him to his cave before his drunken state caused him to stumble into freerise."

Tallow was indignant. "When have any of you known me to consume vision berries? Do I sound as though I'm under their influence now? Check my tongue. Is it stained purple? I'm prepared to take any of you to the stone right now to prove my words."

One of the elders lifted his voice above the confused muttering of the tribesmen. "I would like to hear the message written on this stone."

"Why are you entertaining this delusion?" Flint scoffed.

"It would seem to me that hearing the message would help us determine the plausibility of what Tallow is saying."

Tallow didn't wait for permission to speak. He shared how the Luminaries had been lying to them about the hoisting, cutting the tethers of the elders. He told them of their history as explained by the tinker and offered to show the tinker's drawings. The tribesmen were in an uproar, some denying Tallow's words and others asking questions.

Primelink Flint shouted for silence. "I'm surprised that Tallow didn't share this with me earlier. I wonder why he kept it from me, and I also wonder why he would believe the words of an outsider to undermine our way of life. This is the first I'm hearing of these latest allegations. If such a thing were true, wouldn't we know about it by now?"

Tallow reached for his pack to pull out the photographs. Flint grabbed his arm to stop him. "We've had quite enough of your drawings, Tallow. Everyone here knows you are a talented artist. I won't allow you to use your fanciful sketches as evidence. These drawings are merely your hand's attempt to further your narrative. This isn't proof of anything. You seek to claim my staff by sowing seeds of doubt. Implausible seeds at that."

Tallow ground his teeth. "I've already offered to lead you to the stone. I need no more proof than that." Tallow held a piton aloft. "This is a signature for the Blackspike Tribe. You all recognize it at a glance. It's unique among the tether tribes. One of our spiral pitons is embedded in the stone on the other side of the limen. Follow me there and ask yourself how it made the crossing. Before we get there, ask yourself some other questions —."

Tallow continued before Flint could interrupt him again. "Have any of you ever observed an elder leave on the sky lift? I know you haven't. Don't you find it suspicious that the tribe always numbers thirty? If one of us retires or dies, a wedding occurs, followed by a child shortly after. If a plague befalls us and six of us die, six weddings and six new members replace those who were lost. I have learned that it takes nine months for a child to be born, and several years more before it can leave its mother. Yet we have never waited that long to receive a child capable of speaking and feeding himself.

"All of our life, we've been taught that our brides cannot remain on the surface. We're told that it's for their own protection, but the Luminaries readily place children in our care who can barely cling to a tether. How is it possible that such a young male is able to survive at the base of the swath while a fully grown woman can't? I have seen a woman, as I've already testified, and I can tell you that she's not as fragile as we've been told is the case for her gender. In fact, the woman I met travelled to the limen on her own, with no fear of the beasts we've seen beyond the threshold."

Eyes widened at the mention of the beasts. Many of the tribesmen had watched from the safety of the swath as carnivores took their prey. Those who hadn't witnessed the vicious attacks for themselves were familiar with the gruesome details.

Flint paused for a moment before responding, looking each

tribesmen in the eye. "Which do you think more likely—that our entire way of life has been a lie, or that the Tellusans have filled Tallow's head with lies? The Vigil warned me that the Tellusans are untrustworthy. They're our enemies."

Tallow jumped on those remarks. "The tether tribes have never concerned themselves with external politics. How is it that we have enemies?"

"Perhaps not in the past," Flint countered, "but the Vigil warned me that the Tellusans have been patrolling the limen looking for a way to cross over and attack us."

Shouts of alarm and frantic questions clamoured for attention. "Why are we only hearing of this now?"

Flint ordered the tribe to silence once more. "The Tellusans hope to hurt the Luminaries by cutting off access to the resources we provide. They hope to do this by destroying us. We didn't ask for this fight, but it's coming to us nonetheless."

"How?" Someone shouted. "They can't cross the limen any more than we can."

Flint motioned for calm. "Vigil Strom says that the Tellusans have burrowing machines that can attack us unseen from below the surface."

Worried faces scanned the ground.

"Do not worry, the Luminaries will protect us." Flint assured them. "They've been friends to the tether tribes for generations and they are not ignoring our plight."

"What kind of friends lie?" Tallow pressed. "What kind of friends kill and manipulate? The tinker told me that the Tellusans have no such thing as a burrowing machine, but the Luminaries do have something they call a bomb. It's a device that can cover this entire camp in flames."

"How can we believe such claims?" Bull asked. "We know nothing of these Tellusans."

"I just returned from a scouting mission demanded by the Vigil." Tallow shook his head in disbelief. "I'm still asking myself why our primelink is taking orders from Vigil Strom. That's troubling enough, but not nearly so much as the reason for his loyalty to Vigil Strom. I was asked to place a buoy where I found the granddaughter of Trapper."

"Why?" another elder asked.

"I believe Primelink Flint can answer that question."

Flint saw what Tallow was doing. He was forcing Flint to answer questions that seemed to verify Tallow's version of events. Unfortunately, he couldn't avoid answering without appearing as though he was hiding something. The entire tribe was staring at him. "It's as I said, the Luminaries are our allies. They will send their defenders to that location to protect us from attack by the Tellusans."

"Don't stop there, Flint. Tell us, how will the Luminaries do that?"

Flint was seething at Tallow's disrespectful tone. "They will attack the Tellusans before they can attack us."

"How?" Tallow repeated.

Flint answered with a smug grin. "They will rain fire down on our enemies."

"You mean bombs." Tallow clarified. "We don't know for certain if the Tellusans have burrowing machines, but we do know that our so-called friends have bombs. We don't know for certain if death can come from below the surface, but we do know it can rain down from the sky on either side of the limen."

Eyes turned nervously to the sky.

"The Tellusans I met are simple farmers. They harvest as we do. The Luminaries plan to destroy an entire village of innocent people, including the descendants of our own kin. The Luminaries are the provocateurs. We have always remained apart, but now we're complicit. The Luminaries are dragging us into a conflict of their own making and are turning us into enemies of the Tellusans. Flint could have refused. Instead, he picked a side and chose to follow the Vigil's orders. I'm warning you in advance not to accept an offer of the hoisting when that day comes. You will be led to your death."

"Enough, you troubler!" Flint roared. "The enemy has brainwashed you and you are needlessly frightening the tribe. Everything is well in hand. The Luminaries will keep us safe and life will return to normal." Flint pointed at Tallow and turned to the tribe. "Don't listen to this man's propaganda. The Tellusan woman has tricked him into thinking he can obtain a wife before his time. If he can't have the staff of leadership, then he intends to discredit our way of life, hoping you'll follow him into the wilderness."

"Would that be so bad?" Tallow shot back. "Every tribesman struggles, waiting for a bride while avoiding the taboo of an incestuous relationship. We have no idea who among us may be a biological son or brother and the Luminaries deny us that information. To deal with the forced abstinence, many of us turn to the temporary impotence offered by chewing on tarma leaves. I can't be the only one who hates the unpleasant side effects. Why do we put up with it?

"We don't need the Luminaries for anything other than brides and children—two things we shouldn't have to rely on them to provide. We labour toward that hope, but have no say over when or if we will attain it. The Luminaries have that hold over us and now they drag us into conflict against our will. Flint claims they're our allies, but they have done nothing to earn our trust."

Some of the men were nodding, but others looked uncertain, eyes flicking back and forth between Flint and Tallow. They'd been asked to consider unthinkable things.

"Any one of us could cross the limen tomorrow and search for a bride without blindly trusting the Luminaries who have shown their true colours. As for the rest of my words, you can discover the truth for yourselves by visiting the stone of witness. I will draw you maps or lead you there myself. You have nothing to lose by making the journey."

"You're a traitor to our people and our ways. Bull," Flint commanded, "confine Tallow to his cave. We'll wait to hear what the Vigil has to say about these accusations. We'll learn the truth soon enough."

Bull looked uncomfortable but did as he was told, albeit with less force than on the previous occasion.

"Everything is changing!" Tallow yelled, as he was escorted away. "Whether you like it or not, life will not return to the way it was. Don't trust the Vigil. He doesn't care about us. Seek the truth for yourselves!"

11

His ears were still burning from the tongue-lashing Vigil Strom unleashed. Flint wouldn't admit it to anyone, but he was terrified of the man.

The Vigil was furious. Apparently, Tallow had been spreading his rhetoric to a neighbouring tribe. They had believed his tales, started a rebellion against the Luminaries, and destroyed the base of the sky lift at their camp.

Strom had been very clear that if Flint didn't deal with the problem, brides would be withheld from the Blackspike Tribe. The Vigil's rage was now his own, and he directed it at Tallow. *I've worked too hard to get where I am, I won't let Tallow keep me from obtaining the first wife. I will not allow him to deny me the honour of an early hoisting.*

Flint wasn't sure how to deal with Tallow, so he'd play it by ear. One thing was certain, he wasn't going to let things get worse than they already were. He leaped from his cave to the nearest tree, sinking his knives into the bark with a satisfying thunk. Flint needed to expend some of the tension and anger that had been building since the Vigil left, so he chose not to use the ladder bridges. Five trees later, he was at the entrance to Tallow's cave. "Leave!" Flint barked at Bull. "I want to talk to Tallow alone." He wasn't going to let his people hear any more of Tallow's nonsense.

Flint stormed into the cave, pausing long enough for his eyes to adjust. Tallow was sitting on his sleeping mat, sketching as if he didn't have a care in the world. "You!" He bellowed. Flint ripped the sketch from Tallow's hand and stared at it. His eyes widened as he saw a map to the stone of witness. A stack of similar drawings sat on the sleeping mat next to Tallow. "Even now, as you wait for my decision, you continue with your plans to deceive the tribe?"

Tallow looked at him calmly. "I've only told you the truth. I don't want to lose any more of our brothers to the heartless machinations of the Luminaries. You hold a map in your hand. You can go see the truth for yourself."

"I forbade you from talking to the Tellusans, yet you did so anyway. They filled your head with lies which you've carried home, like a plague of the mind. You disobeyed me again! Why? Why do you constantly goad me?"

"I know you believe so, even though I've never defied you before. I do so now only because the lives of others depend on my speaking up."

"We know nothing of Tellusan ways, but we know the Vigil. The Vigil says that the Tellusans are deceivers. Our way of life includes the Luminaries, as it has been from the beginning. Haven't they faithfully brought us brides? Haven't they traded fairly with us? Those gauntlets on your arms are courtesy of luminary craftsman. You've spoken briefly with one Tellusan woman and you're ready to throw it all away? You're risking our heritage and displeasing our allies."

"Allies? Flint, a major part of our heritage is our isolation. We remain apart from the rest of the world. We don't take sides in external conflicts. Don't you find it strange that the Vigil is making demands and telling you to enter a conflict with the Tellusans? Why are you allowing the Vigil to change our ways? The truth is that luminary actions have threatened our heritage for some time, without any help from me."

"It's not that simple. The Tellusans are about to invade. If we don't stop them here and now, our tribe and all of our ways will cease to exist. If that means we need to bend a little for a short time, then so be it. We need all tether tribes to rally together, but you've been interfering with that as well, haven't you? The Vigil told me that a neighbouring tether tribe has threatened the Luminaries and destroyed their sky lift! They were making the same accusations as you are."

"Good for them! At least someone is taking this seriously."

"Do you have any idea what you've done, Tallow? The Luminaries are threatening to withhold brides because of your actions. Even if you were right about everything, you've condemned us all!"

Tallow rose to his feet. "They can't do that! We've paid for their care in advance. Why aren't you fighting for us, Flint? What more proof do you need that the Luminaries are controlling us? What happened to you?"

"Don't you dare try to blame me! This is all your fault. We used to do everything together. You pushed me—challenged me—made me better. When I slipped, you'd catch me. We supported each other. I always knew you had my back—until you didn't. After I was voted primelink, you abandoned me. I wanted you as my second, but you refused. You rejected me and began to undermine me. I've put up with it for years, but you've crossed a line, Tallow. I'm giving you an opportunity to make things right. Tell the tribe you were lying to them."

"I can't do that, Flint. They need to know the truth. I've never lied to them or you. Why won't you believe me? I'm begging you. If the friendship we once shared meant anything to you, visit the stone."

Flint felt his fingers tighten on the climbing knives in his hands. "I can think of an easier way to find out if you're telling the truth. All we need to do is wait for the next hoisting ceremony and we can watch the elders rise on the sky lift. I noticed you never suggested that option. Why? Is it because you're trying to lead the tribe into a trap? How many Tellusans are waiting at this stone of yours?"

"What? No! It's not a trap, it's just the fastest way to the truth. It could be years before the next hoisting ceremony. We can't wait that long." Tallow slowly shook his head. "You've changed, Flint. I've seen it coming for a long time, but you've finally descended into full-blown paranoia. You're not fit to lead."

A growl passed Flint's lips and he gnashed his teeth, biting the inside of his cheek in the process. He could taste blood, the pain fuelling his rising ire. "I suppose you think that *you're* fit to lead in my stead? I always knew you coveted my position. I believe I'm hearing truth from your lips for the first time." Flint lowered his voice to a menacing timbre. "This is your last chance. Will you tell the tribe you were lying to them, or not?"

"No, Flint, I refuse to play along with whatever it is you and the Luminaries have planned. You've made your bed. Now you can lie in it, but I'll do my best to make sure the rest of the tribe doesn't climb under the covers with you."

"You treacherous backstabber!" Flint roared. "Your sedition ends here and now!" Flint leaped at Tallow, knives flashing.

Tallow dodged one blade but the second found his shoulder. The two of them collided and crashed into the cave wall, flesh scraping against the rough surface. Tallow was gripping Flint's wrists, struggling to hold the primelink's knives at bay. Flint had always been the stronger of the two, and he slowly forced his knives toward Tallow's throat. "I can't believe I put up with you for as long as I did—no more!"

Pain exploded behind Flint's eyes as Tallow's forehead smashed into his nose. He stumbled back and Tallow took that moment to flee from the cave. Flint regained his senses and leaped after him. One of the knives flew from his hand with near deadly accuracy. It sailed just past Tallow's head and embedded into a tree as he shifted out of the knife's path. Flint pulled a spare from his belt and dove toward a different tree along an intercept course. "Come back and face your punishment, you coward!"

It was a reckless chase, neither of them bothering with pitons. Sooner or later one of them would make a fatal mistake. Flint was counting on it being Tallow, but his new gauntlets were serving him well and he'd had much more practice moving through the forest at speed. Tallow's lead grew. *Catching him will be impossible now,* Flint thought. "This isn't over, Tallow!" He yelled, "I'll find you and then we'll finish this!"

Flint gasped for breath as he clung to a tree and placed a piton. It was maddening that Tallow had escaped, but he couldn't think about that right now. He needed to get back to the tribe and try to clean up the mess Tallow had left behind.

***

Tallow couldn't believe that Flint tried to kill him. *What do I do now? I can't ever go home. Both Flint and Vigil Strom will be waiting for me, and I don't need to guess what the outcome will be.*

Tallow decided his best bet was to visit the Fleetwood Tether Tribe. If they destroyed their sky lift, then the Luminaries couldn't come after him there. It would give him a little time to decide what to do. *I'd also like to see if anything happened at the location where I released the buoy.* Formulating a plan as he continued on, Tallow knew he needed to produce proper maps to record the things he heard and saw. All of it was evidence that might help convince others one day. He needed to get his hands on more paper and writing instruments. The Fleetwood Tribe could provide that and provision him with other necessities as well. He'd left everything behind in his cave. Luckily, he was wearing his gauntlets. Unfortunately, he only had a few pitons clipped to his vest, the rest were in his travel bag back at the cave.

If he could locate his original path, he would find pitons in the trees from his previous journey. If not, he'd need to rely on some old slipknot techniques for tying the safety tether around a tree branch. It was a tedious process that didn't always work and sometimes required going back to the original tree to reclaim a stubborn tether. It would add weeks to his travels, and without supplies, he'd need to find a way to nourish himself on the journey.

Tallow took stock. His harness held a small snare and a few strips of dried meat. He had his knives as well as his gauntlets and spurs, but nothing to hold water. His first order of business would be to find a wild gourd, or some bamboo segments that would hold water, and then he'd snare a few rodents. Edible berries or other fruits and tubers were always available, but foraging would slow him a great deal until he could build up some stores. Tallow sighed as he set himself to his new task. Much as he hated the delay, he didn't really have a choice.

***

As Tallow neared the Fleetwood Tribe's encampment, he stopped at the river to fill his gourd. He hadn't noticed while he was noisily leaping through the forest, but now that he'd stopped, the surrounding quiet was unnerving. Insects were still making their presence known, but birdsong and the ever-present chittering of other tree dwelling creatures was missing. It felt unnatural, raising goosebumps on his arms. He continued on, but slowed his advance. Tallow made shorter leaps, closer to the bases of larger trees, reducing the noise of his passage.

Before long the scent of burnt foliage hit him and he gave up all attempts at stealth. Flying recklessly through the trees, Tallow almost stumbled into freerise when he suddenly ran out of targets. He managed to grab a branch of the tree he had just sprung from. Pulling himself back to safety, he surveyed the area in shock. The Fleetwood camp no longer existed. All that remained were charred and smouldering stumps. *The Luminaries... They can rain fire from the sky.* This was retribution for the Fleetwood Tribe's rebellion. If anyone needed proof that the Luminaries were unscrupulous, here it was. The picture Sicily had placed in his mind when she described a bomb was nowhere near as horrifying as the reality.

Tallow swallowed hard as a tear streaked down his face. *This is my fault. I should have warned them to leave.* Even as he thought it, he realized that it wouldn't have occurred to him. They'd been comfortable in their seclusion for so long, they had no way to gauge a threat of this nature. The tether tribes were completely unaware of what the Luminaries were literally holding over their heads. Tallow felt like he was going to be sick, but his stomach was as empty as the scene before him. He'd used up the last of his supplies believing he would find food and shelter here.

Tallow stared at the bleakness for several hours. Whenever a gust of wind dislodged a flake of charcoal, another piece of the Fleetwood Tether Tribe flew to heaven. Eventually, he noticed a piton in a nearby tree at the edge of the ruin. Without thinking, he retrieved that remnant and clipped it to his vest. The action settled into resolve. *I will make sure the world knows what happened here.* With that conviction firmly entrenched, Tallow went about the gruesome task of searching the remains for anything that might be useful in furthering that goal.

12

Arlo Leonis burst into Lomar's workshop. "Mr. Romero! She's getting ready to leave again!"

Lomar hired the boy to keep an eye on Sicily. His ego was still stinging from her aversion to his marriage proposal. Even so, he was willing to forgive her. He'd spent a great deal of time planning out his future and decided that Sicily would make the most suitable wife. It would also help to justify the money he'd spent on her father's debt. That decision was strictly an investment opportunity, but it was always pleasant when several ventures came together.

Lomar tried to help her see the logic in their union, but she hadn't come around. It was confusing to him. She possessed no right to property or inheritance, and when her father died, she would find herself destitute in a remote village with limited employment opportunities. Without a benefactor, she would be reduced to foraging in the wilderness or some other distasteful means of supporting herself. In fact, Lomar had already been that benefactor for her family without her knowledge. Now that she knew, she seemed indignant and unwilling to continue accepting the help he'd already been providing. It was utterly baffling to him.

Her resistance to the inevitable suggested she might have the means to provide for herself, some source that he was unaware of. Lomar couldn't imagine what that might be. It had come to his attention that she would disappear for hours at a time and no one seemed to know where she went. Lomar had seen her talking to Adis, the tinker. He was the one person who might see her safely to another village, but as Lomar knew from experience, the tinker wouldn't provide his services for free. It was possible the tinker would consider trading his services for something of value. If Sicily possessed something worth enough to provide her with the financial means to procure both a mount and passage, then it was something Lomar would be very interested in—from a business standpoint, if nothing else. Prospects of financial gain aside, he found Sicily pleasing to the eye and would be disappointed if she left.

Sicily was up to something and Lomar disliked remaining in the dark. He prided himself on knowing everything that happened in Endelton. Arlo kept him apprised of her movements, and learned that she would complete her milk deliveries early on the days that she disappeared. She was preparing to leave on one of her mysterious journeys, and this time he was ready to follow her.

Lomar closed up shop and jogged to Sicily's farm, ducking behind a shed in time to see her leaving. She carried nothing but a walking stick. She didn't appear to be prepared for work of any kind. Lomar grew more curious by the moment and silently shadowed her from a safe distance. He'd find out what this was about, modifying his plans for their future as necessary.

***

Sicily walked briskly to the stone of witness. Clouds stretched across the sky in long wispy tendrils and a light breeze swayed the tall grasses that ran up to the treeline along the limen. She glanced over her shoulder to make sure no one was following her. Trapper's stone was a family secret. Her grandfather worried someone might deface it before it accomplished the goal he had in mind. It wasn't all that far from the village, but unless you had directions or were patrolling the limen for some reason, it was unlikely anyone would come across it by chance. A stranger would have no reason to wander in this remote locale, and the townsfolk were too busy to waste their time exploring her family's fields. Still, she was cautious out of habit and entered the treeline well to the west of her final destination.

The stone sat in a small clearing among the trees, creating a sheltered area. Her grandfather had planted some shrubs around the stone, so it wasn't easily visible unless you were on the swath side of the limen. A fallen log lay nearby where Sicily liked to sit when she visited this place. It was a good spot to be alone with her thoughts, which inevitably wandered to her family history.

Life had not been easy for her grandfather when he first wandered into Endelton. Trust was not easy to come by in a frontier town. He'd sat on the outskirts for days, watching the villagers who eyed him with suspicion. He seemed lost and bewildered. His thin frame and lack of weapons made him more of a curiosity than a threat. The town had discussed what to do about the matter and decided to leave him alone until the tinker arrived with some kind of legal precedent. It was then that her grandmother decided to speak with him.

When she drew near and saw his malnourished state, she immediately took him to her home and fed him. As time passed and he gained his strength, she learned more about who and what he was. The stories of his tribe enthralled her, as did his striking features. They fell in love and she taught him Tellusan ways. To hear the story from her grandmother's lips, it was a fairy tale come to life. Sicily had grown up with those stories, longing to learn more about the outside world and to have the kind of happiness her grandparents shared. It was romantic nonsense, she knew, but a part of her hoped to have that with Tallow.

Perhaps today would be the day that Tal returned. It was no surprise that other tether tribesmen failed to appear on their own over the past several weeks. If Tal had successfully warned his people, she suspected they would arrive together. She had no doubt that he'd stop here first, if only to say goodbye. The arrival of Tal's people wouldn't necessarily indicate a desire to cross the limen. It could simply mean that they were striking out on their own, far away from luminary control.

I wonder if Tal has decided to make the crossing? Between herself and the tinker, she felt they had done much to dispel any myths about the risk of crossing over. However, a fear remained of leaving everything he knew for a life as an outsider. He had no guarantee of acceptance. In most major cities, he would be viewed as one of the Aerish. That would carry an unavoidable stigma, one she hadn't warned him about. Sicily suddenly felt guilty for wanting him to take her someplace that would make his life even more difficult than in Endelton. At least here they had come to accept her grandfather and would likely extend that same courtesy to Tal— eventually.

The sound of a twig snapping ended Sicily's contemplation. She couldn't tell where the sound originated. *Did someone follow me?* She thought she'd been careful. She rose and cautiously began to walk the perimeter of the little clearing, peering through the trees.

"Sicily."

She jumped—heart thumping, and with her hand on her chest, began to laugh as she recognized Tal's voice. "Don't startle me like that!"

"I'm sorry, Sicily."

"No, it's okay, I'm glad you're here." Sicily peered past him into the treetops beyond. "Did any of your brothers join you?"

Tallow's face darkened. "I didn't have time to convince them. Vigil Strom has poisoned the primelink's mind. He imprisoned me again and when I refused to stop warning the tribe, he tried to kill me."

Sicily brought her hands to her face in shock. "Oh, Tal—I'm so sorry." It was then that she spotted the angry scar on his shoulder.

Tallow noticed her gaze. "I was lucky—unlike the Fleetwood Tribe."

"Fleetwood Tribe?"

Tallow shook his head. He tried to speak but choked on his words. After a brief pause, he tried again. "When I left to place the buoy, I ran into a scout from a neighbouring tether tribe—the Fleetwood Tribe. I told them all that I had learned, sharing the tinker's photos with them. It turns out our two tribes share the same Vigil. Primelink Longshadow wasn't happy with the Vigil's recent requests and staged a rebellion."

"A rebellion? How does a tether tribe of a few dozen men stage a rebellion against the Luminaries?" Sicily wondered aloud.

"The Fleetwood Tribe chose to show their displeasure by destroying the base of the sky lift."

Sicily's eyes widened. "Whoa—that would do it. How did the Luminaries respond?"

"They rained fire on the tribe."

"They didn't!" Sicily gasped. "I can't believe they would take that risk. If other nations find out, there will be consequences."

"After Flint chased me from my home, I sought refuge with the Fleetwood Tether Tribe. When I arrived at their camp, it was gone. They were wiped from existence. All that remains is a charred black stain. From there, I travelled to the location of the buoy. An even larger black scar stains the Tellusan landscape a mile in width and several miles long. Had I not seen it with my own eyes, I would have trouble believing the destructive potential of a bomb. The land is devoid of life and covered in craters."

"Adis was right." Sicily breathed.

"Speaking of the tinker, have you heard from him? I'm worried he may have been too close to the conflagration."

"I have not, but he's due back at Endelton in the next few days."

Sicily moved closer and looked deep into Tallow's eyes. He seemed lost and she wondered if her grandmother had seen something similar in her grandfather's eyes when they first met. "What will you do, Tal? Where will you go?"

"There's no place left for me in the swath. I don't know of any other tether tribes nearby, and a search for them could take years. I'm unwilling to live on my own for such a long time."

Sicily silently searched his face, unwilling to threaten her hope with words. She refused to make that mistake a second time.

"I'm not ready to give up on my people, but I need more proof. How can I ask them to consider something I haven't done myself? So, I've decided to cross the limen first, and then see if I can convince them to do the same."

Sicily let go of the breath she'd been holding, a smile spreading across her face. "When?"

"I see little point in waiting. How do we do this?"

Sicily wrung her hands, not wanting to show her eagerness, but worried he might change his mind if she tarried. It would be easy enough for Tal to access the tree her grandfather had planted as a bridge, but maybe she could further allay his fears. "Can you throw one end of your tether to me through the limen?"

Tallow searched the surface on his side until he spotted the tip of a buried rock. He quickly dug it out and fastened it to the end of his tether. "I'll need to throw it with some force, so I'll aim to your right. Are you ready?"

Sicily nodded and he heaved the stone toward the limen. It made a confused wobble as it passed through and landed a few feet away. She quickly untied the tether from the rock and ran to the stone of witness. It seemed appropriate that her grandfather should somehow be involved in this historic moment. "I'm going to clip this end of your tether to the piton embedded in Grandfather's stone. Clip the other end to your harness. It should provide some additional safety as you cross. The tree straddles both sides of the limen. All you need to do is use the tree as a bridge. Once you've climbed to one of the lower branches on this side, you can drop down."

Tallow nodded and clipped the tether to his vest. He leaped to the bridge tree and carefully plotted his route among the branches.

Sicily picked up some of the slack in the tether and wrapped it around her forearm. "I'll hold on to the tether as well, just in case."

Tallow smiled and Sicily blushed. It would be impossible for her to anchor his weight if something went wrong—they both knew it, but he didn't laugh and it meant the world that he trusted her.

Tallow moved cautiously, making sure his gauntlets were secure with every tiny progression. A moment of panic temporarily crossed his face as he pulled his head across the turbulent plane of the threshold. He struggled to reorient himself as the pull of gravity reversed. Half of his body pulled in one direction and half in the other. The struggle seemed to solidify his resolve, and he quickly traversed the remaining distance. Tallow clung to the stout branch, fully on the Tellusan side of the limen, but he hesitated, unwilling to let go. He could feel the downward pull of gravity toward the surface, but it went against everything in his nature to believe that he would fall in that direction. Then Sicily was there—reaching toward him.

She smiled at him, encouraging him with her eyes. "Get a good grip and let your legs dangle."

Tallow wrapped his arms around the limb with a death grip and slowly lowered his legs to within reach of Sicily.

"I'm just going to remove these spurs, so I don't cut myself, okay?"

Tallow nodded, but said nothing.

Sicily wrapped her arms around his legs and looked up at him. "Okay, unwrap your arms. Just use your hands and lower yourself some more."

Tallow hesitated before doing as she asked.

Sicily wrapped her arms tightly around Tallow's waist and steadied her legs into a solid stance. "I've got you, Tal. I know it doesn't feel right to you, but trust me. You know I'm anchored to the ground and you're anchored to me. Let go of the branch."

Tallow didn't move.

"Sooner or later you're going to tire out and lose your grip. Then you'll fall anyway."

Tallow let out a strangled yell and released his grip. His slim frame was heavier than Sicily expected and they tumbled to the ground as Tallow fell into her arms. He didn't move for a moment and then he clung to her fiercely, burrowing his face into her neck. The emotions of recent events caught up with him, and he began to weep.

Sicily held tightly, allowing him the release he'd not allowed himself. Tallow had lost his brothers, the only family he'd ever known. Tallow's history and way of life were gone. An entire tribe had died because of the truth he'd shared with them. Now he was a stranger in a strange land at the mercy of a woman he barely knew—the very woman who had caused all of his problems in the first place. Sicily couldn't begin to understand what he was going through—or maybe she could. The scope was different, but her mother had died when she needed her most. In a way, she'd lost her family identity on that day. Nothing had ever been the same. Hadn't she been misled, living a lie as her father gambled away her inheritance and her future? And what about the men who were trying to control her life by robbing her of options? She felt lost too, and tears sprang to her eyes, mingling with Tallow's.

They held each other until no more tears came and then, Tallow kissed her. Tentative at first, and then hungrily. Sicily knew then that she was as much of a lifeline for him as he had become for her.

"Unhand her!"

Sicily looked around in confusion. A figure was looming over her, blocking out the sun. Shading her eyes with her hand, Sicily tried to make out the features of the shadow above her. "Lomar! What are you doing here? Are you following me?"

"I was worried about you, Sicily. I came to your house and saw you heading into the wilderness alone with nothing but a walking stick. I thought to provide an escort, but then I lost sight of you. I feared some wild beast might attack you, and I see now that I was right! Get off her, you cad!"

Lomar pulled a knife from the sheath at his waist and took a step toward Tallow.

Sicily scrambled to her feet and stepped in front of him. "Lomar, you're mistaken. This man was not attacking me."

"Mistaken? A half-naked man had you pinned to the ground with his lips over your mouth while tears streamed down your cheeks." Lomar pushed past her. "Run home and lock the doors, Sicily. I'll take care of this— ruffian."

Tallow struggled to his feet, unsteady in the heavier gravity. Lomar lunged at him and Sicily held her breath in horror as the knife speared toward Tallow's stomach. At the last second, Tallow dodged with surprising speed. His muscles were weaker, but his reflexes remained quick.

Lomar seemed surprised as he reassessed his opponent, slowly withdrawing a second knife and advancing again.

"Lomar, stop!" Sicily yelled, "He's my..." What could she say? They hadn't had time to discuss what they meant to each other. " ... he's my friend." She finished lamely.

Lomar spun on her. "Your friend? A man who tries to take advantage of you in the dirt? Are you so desperate for affection that you'd defend this vagrant?"

"How dare you! If I'm so desperate, ask yourself why I didn't run to your bedchambers the moment you offered a bride price. Tal wasn't attacking me and he's not a vagrant. I — I love him!"

"You're confused, Sicily, perhaps you've had too much sun. You can't possibly expect me to believe that you would choose this uncivilized tribesman over me."

"I would and I do!"

Lomar sneered as he turned back to Tallow. "I won't let you throw your life away, Sicily."

Lomar roared in frustration and threw himself at Tallow, swinging with both knives. Tallow evaded the first blow and would have deflected the second with his gauntlet, but he fell to the ground as he stumbled over a rock. Lomar was on him in a second, pinning him to the ground. He lifted his blade to strike. Tallow unsheathed his gauntlets and slashed out instinctively, catching Lomar across the side of his head. At the same time, Sicily launched herself at Lomar, catching him in the ribs and knocking him off Tallow.

Lomar glared at Sicily as he found his feet, hand covering the wound on his head. He pulled his hand away, surprised to see it covered in blood. Three ugly slashes carved his face from ear to mouth, just below his right eye. Lomar still held a knife in his right hand, and he pointed it at Tallow. "You'll regret this, stranger."

Tallow stood his ground, waiting for another attack. Lomar glanced at the gauntlets and backed away. When he'd moved a sufficient distance, he turned and slowly made his way back to the village, one hand clutching his ribs and the other his face.

"Are you hurt?" Sicily turned Tallow this way and that, looking for wounds.

Tallow found her hands and settled them. "You love me?"

"I shouldn't have said that, I'm sorry."

"Did you mean it?"

Sicily felt her face heating, but didn't want to deny her feelings anymore. "Yes," She whispered.

Tallow lifted her chin and kissed her gently. "I love you, too. Even if your friends are bloodthirsty lunatics."

Sicily smiled and pulled him close. She didn't know what the future would bring, but she no longer felt alone.

13

Tallow chose to remain at the stone of witness for the time being. He'd crossed back and forth across the limen, familiarizing himself with the process. It wasn't long before he could traverse the tree bridge quickly and safely. Sicily had hoped he would come home with her, but Tallow argued that she needed to speak with her father before dropping a tribesman on the doorstep. Tallow also felt more comfortable spending his nights in the swath. The thought of a wild beast attacking him in his sleep was a persistent fear, despite Sicily's assurance that such a thing was highly unlikely.

Give him time, this is all new to him.

Sicily was delivering milk when she heard a commotion in the village square. As she drew near, she could see a large crowd had formed. It appeared that the whole village had assembled. Even the field workers had left their chores. Sicily looked around for her father and moved to his side when she spotted him.

"What's going on, Papa?"

"Your guess is as good as mine. Lomar called an emergency meeting."

Sure enough, Lomar was standing on the courtyard stage next to the mayor, a portion of his face covered by a bandana.

Mayor Hawton raised his hands for silence, and a hush fell on the crowd. "I'm sure you're all wondering about the reason for this emergency meeting. Mr. Romero is concerned for the safety of our village. We're still gathering information, but considering Lomar's injuries, I'm inclined to err on the side of caution. Lomar will say a few words and then if any of you have additional information to share, please come see me afterwards."

The air began to buzz with whispered speculation as more people noticed Lomar's bandana covered face.

"Good people of Endelton. I've come to warn you of a dire threat. We've always been an isolated community far from the concerns that plague some of the big cities. Indeed many of us moved here for that very reason. We've enjoyed peace and safety for many years, but now that coveted peace is threatened. We're not as isolated as we believed."

Murmurs rippled through the audience. "What are you talking about, Romero? Get to the point. The fields are standing empty while you exercise your jawbone."

Lomar held up a placating hand. "I'm talking about invaders at our doorstep."

"Have you been sampling the Marin brother's wine?" That brought a round of laughter.

"I'm talking about the tether tribes."

"Are you daft, man? Old Trapper lived among us for years—or have you forgotten? He was a tribesman and never gave us cause to fear. He told us the nearest tether tribe was far from here."

"That was many years ago. We have no idea what the tribes are like now. Besides, if I'm not mistaken, Trapper left his tribe because he was fleeing death. Or have *you* forgotten? Don't think for a moment that we're safe from the violence that tether tribes are capable of. If Trapper crossed the limen, others can follow. In fact, I saw a tribesman on this side of the limen not two days ago."

Voices rose, demanding answers. Mayor Hawton shouted for silence. "Let the man speak!"

Lomar nodded his thanks and continued. "As many of you know, I have a vested interest in the Basurto property. I was pacing off the boundaries when I ran into a tribesman southeast of the Basurto homestead. He had Sicily on the ground and was attempting to ravish her. I shudder to think what might have happened if I hadn't arrived in time."

Ryo turned to Sicily, the shock clear on his face. "The tribesman attacked you? Why didn't you tell me?"

"He didn't attack me, Papa."

"But Lomar just said —"

"Quiet, Papa! I'll explain later."

All eyes were on Lomar. "When Trapper was still among us, he explained the way of the tether tribes—how they have no females living among them. I have seen how brazen they've become. They're clearly willing to prey on the women of our village. Where one tribesman lingers, many others lie in wait. This scout knows we're here and will report back to his brothers. I have no doubt they will soon come upon us in force and take for themselves what they desire."

Several of the younger women gasped and huddled together. Men stood protectively nearby. Lomar had struck a nerve, and they were all listening intently. Ryo Basurto turned to Sicily and likewise vowed to protect her.

"I don't need protecting, Papa. There's no invasion."

Sicily forced her way through the crowd and climbed the steps of the stage. "It's true that a tribesman crossed to our side of the limen, but he did not attack me. Lomar is mistaken, this is all a misunderstanding."

"Sicily is in shock. She's playing down events as a defence mechanism. I know what I saw. When I confronted him, he turned his attack on me. If this tribesman came in peace, then why did he do this?"

Lomar pulled the bandana free and revealed three ugly gashes disfiguring his face. The crowd gasped in consternation.

"Make no mistake—these tether tribes are violent aggressors! This one man attacked both Sicily and me. Do you think the rest of you will be spared when they come in force?"

The villagers stared at Lomar, wide-eyed.

"Bring your blades to my shop. If you don't have a blade, bring any implement suitable for use as a weapon. I'll hone the edges for free. If you don't own anything suitable, I'll provide you with a means to defend yourself. We need to prepare and there's no time to waste."

Lomar hopped off the stage. "I see some of the field workers already have items in hand. Follow me!"

The square cleared as people either followed Lomar or rushed to their homes.

Sicily shook her head in disbelief. "I have to warn Tal."

Ryo stepped in front of Sicily to get her attention. "Who's Tal? Sicily, what's going on?"

"I'm sorry, Papa, I meant to tell you sooner. I'm afraid it will have to wait."

Sicily turned to leave, but her father grabbed her wrist. "Sicily, wait. Have you given any more consideration to Lomar's proposal?"

She spun back to face her father who lost his grip on her wrist in the process. "Are you serious, Papa? I've already told you several times that I have no interest in marrying Lomar."

"Surely with everything that's happening, you'll reconsider. Lomar can protect you so much better than I can. Please, Sicily, I don't want to see you hurt by these invaders."

Sicily growled in exasperation. "There is no invasion, Papa! Lomar is lying. He's angry because I rejected him. He wants to hurt the man that I love. Lomar attacked Tal, not the other way around. Tal was only defending himself. Those cuts on Lomar's face are his own fault!"

"You've met a tribesman and you kept it from me? I don't understand how that could have occurred."

Sicily shook her head in disbelief. "You married a woman whose mother experienced the same thing and you have to ask how it's possible? I don't have time for this, Papa, I have to go." Sicily spun and took off at a run for the stone of witness.

14

Tallow smiled as he stood in front of the tinker. The last few days had induced an inexplicable mixture of fear and euphoria. He wasn't sure if he could tell the difference. A week had passed since Lomar attacked him. Sicily filled him in on the events that followed. Lomar had turned the town against Tallow and it didn't seem likely that he could live there as he'd hoped. The situation filled him with despair, however, having set in his mind that Sicily would be part of his future, he couldn't bear the thought of returning to his solitary existence.

Sicily seemed to have other plans. She didn't appear to share his disappointment at their inevitable separation. At first he was confused, but then she explained what she had in mind. Her face turned an adorable shade of pink as she wrung her hands and suggested a way that both of them could escape their respective predicaments. Tallow grinned recalling how she'd apologized at least three times before she actually told him what she was thinking.

With very few options available to Tallow, he was open to Sicily's plan. It certainly seemed less risky than anything he might come up with considering his limited knowledge of Tellusan law. He warmed to the idea as they discussed it further and assured Sicily that he was willing to follow her lead.

Now they stood before Adis, the tinker, who had returned that very morning. Tallow was profoundly relieved that the tinker had not died at the site of the buoy. Adis shared the devastating evidence he had successfully recorded while at the destroyed site. Tallow gaped at the photos showing proof of the Luminary Navy raining bombs across the limen. He felt a familiar shock, once again seeing the destruction Luminaries could precipitate.

"Thank you for your help, Tallow. This will go a long way in our efforts to pressure the Luminaries into granting access to the sky lifts. It's only the first step in exposing the atrocities your people have faced, but the door has been opened and the Tinker's Guild will not let it close again.

"As for the other matter—I would be honoured to preside over your wedding ceremony. Sicily isn't required to marry, she has no legal obligation to her father or Lomar. However, Sicily is correct that they will have no reason to continue pressuring her once she's married to another."

Sicily glanced at Tallow with a shy smile, and he squeezed her hand in response.

"More importantly," Adis continued, "once you're wed, Tallow will officially become a part of the community. The people of Endelton will have to accept him as one of their own. Given time, I'm certain that the villagers will come to realize Tallow is no threat." Adis grew serious. "You'll need to be on your best behaviour for a while, Tallow. Try not to give anyone a legal means to bring charges against you. Sicily will explain our laws, but don't pick fights. As for the confrontation with Lomar—it's his word against Sicily's, but be warned that if you should find yourself in another fight among witnesses, things could turn bad for you. As a government sanctioned mediator, there's only so much I can do to protect you if you accidentally land on the wrong side of the law."

"I'll keep that in mind."

"Please, do. Lomar may try to provoke you. The man has a temper, as I'm sure you've noticed."

Sicily snorted. "That's putting it mildly."

"When would you two like to proceed with this ceremony?"

Sicily looked up at Tallow. "This isn't just a marriage of convenience to me, though I will clearly benefit. Lomar will have to leave me alone, and my peers will no longer be able to blame me for their own relationship problems. I'll also have someone to travel with if we decide to leave Endelton, and you know that's something I've dreamed about. However, I don't want you to feel as if I've pressured you into this. I want you to know that I no longer feel a need to escape. You don't have to protect me. I've learned something about what's important to me—what I thought was a solution to my problems wasn't the answer after all. I can't imagine a life without you and I would still choose you, even if it meant the situations I found myself in got worse rather than better. I want this regardless of the outcome, but you can still change your mind. I'll understand. I know I'm asking more of you than I have any right to ask."

Tallow shook his head and smiled. "I was alone with nowhere to go, this will be a fresh start—a home and a future with the one who captured my heart. I feel as if I'm the one who has the most to gain. As you said, I can't imagine a life without you. There's no place I'd rather be than right here at your side."

"Well," Adis winked, "your declarations sounded like wedding vows to me. I suppose there's no time like the present to complete this ceremony. Give me a moment to gather the legal documents —" Angry shouts interrupted Adis as a crowd approached.

"There he is!" Lomar was leading a mob of weapon brandishing villagers. They began to run toward Tallow, but seemed to think better of it when they noticed the tinker's wagon. Adis stepped in front of Tallow. "What's this all about?"

Lomar pointed a menacing machete at Tallow. "These tribesmen are planning an attack on Endelton. We're patrolling the village. If they try anything, we'll be ready."

"Nothing could be further from the truth, Lomar. I know Tallow and I can vouch for him." Adis looked around at the other villagers. "The Luminaries are oppressing the tether tribes. Tallow is a fleeing refugee who is no danger to you."

At the tinker's words, the villagers lowered their weapons, growing uncertain about their original response to Lomar's incitement.

"How can we know that for certain?" Lomar pressed, "and even if what you say is true, it doesn't excuse the actions of this one." Lomar lifted his chin at Tallow. "I saw him attack Sicily."

Lomar's followers looked to Sicily for confirmation.

"You're telling tales, Lomar! Tal didn't attack me."

"You don't know what you're saying, Sicily." Lomar took in the questioning faces of the men behind him. "Don't you see what's happening here? This tribesman has her under some kind of spell." He turned back to Sicily. "Step away from him, Sicily, you don't have to pretend. I won't let him hurt you. I can protect you."

"I don't need your protection, Lomar. I definitely don't need your marriage proposal. Just leave it be already. I want nothing to do with your plans!" Sicily looked at the other villagers. "Do you need proof that I'm in no danger? You've heard Adis vouch for Tallow. He was preparing to marry us before you interrupted the proceedings. Have you come here to lynch the groom? For what crime? Go back to your homes!"

Lomar's face grew purple with rage. "You ungrateful..." He spun to face the tinker.

"You see what he did to my face. I demand recompense."

Adis shrugged. "As I've said, Tallow is a refugee. He fled the swath and has nothing of value for you to claim."

"The law states an eye for an eye. I demand the right to draw blood."

"That will serve no good purpose, Lomar. Perhaps we can work out an arrangement for Tallow to repay your grievances with labour."

"I don't want his help. I want his blood." Lomar stepped forward menacingly.

"I'm sorry, Tallow," Adis whispered, "It's his legal right, but he can't do more than draw blood. Try to allow him a minor cut and then I can quickly call this to an end." Adis stepped back, pulling a struggling Sicily with him.

Tallow faced his opponent with a look of disbelief at the pronouncement.

The villagers surrounded the two combatants as Lomar took a swing at Tallow's midsection.

Tallow dodged and the blade whistled past.

This is crazy, I'm not going to let him cut me. I've done nothing wrong!

Lomar pulled a second blade from a sheath on his back and began to swing wildly. Tallow felt the weight of extra gravity on his frame, but he'd grown accustomed to the pull and still had his reflexes. Lomar was sweating from exertion and continued to fail in his attempts to land a blow.

Maybe he'll tire himself out and give up.

Lomar directed another swing at Tallow's head. He fell into a crouch and hooked his foot behind Lomar's knee, bringing him to the ground. Lomar lost one of his swords in the process. Grabbing a handful of dirt, Lomar threw it in Tallow's eyes as he rose to his feet.

Tallow grunted as he fell to his knees trying to wipe the stinging soil from his eyes. He only managed to irritate them more. *I can't see!* Tallow panicked, having no confidence that Lomar would be satisfied with inflicting just a small wound. He heard a growl and footsteps running toward him. Tallow reflexively unsheathed the claws on his gauntlets and threw his arms into the air in an attempt to block what he couldn't see coming. He felt resistance as his claws swung upwards.

Lomar screamed in pain and the villagers gasped. Tallow scooted backwards on hands and feet, his eyes watering. When he reached the tinker's wagon, he stood and looked around. As his eyes began to clear, he took in the angry expressions of the townsfolk. Lomar was on his knees clutching his bleeding chest which sported several new cuts. Tallow's eyes widened in fear. Wounding Lomar further had not been his intent.

"I'll kill you!" Lomar yelled. He turned to the residents of Endelton. "Do you still think this man is innocent? He refuses to abide by our laws. Instead, he attacks me again! He holds no regard for the citizens of this town. It's as I said. He's the first of many invaders to come. We must protect ourselves!"

Endelton was normally a peaceful place, violence was rare. The blood running freely from Lomar's wounds was shocking to the witnesses. The expressions on their faces transformed from horror to fear and then to anger. They began to shout as they advanced on Tallow.

Adis stepped forward and raised his hands. "Stop! You know the law. Where an accused man faces the ire of an entire community, he's bestowed the right to flight. The law grants him a head start, leaving a gap for the will of God to condemn or impart freedom. Tallow needs to know his rights. Give me a few minutes to explain them to him."

Adis pulled Tallow aside and whispered, "I once witnessed this kind of mob mentality in another village. Stopping them will be difficult and I have no legal grounds to interfere. It's not a law I agree with, but it's the law in these parts, nonetheless. Listen carefully. If you manage to escape, meet me back at the stone of witness in two weeks' time. Once the dust has settled, I may be able to help."

The mob grew restless as Adis spoke with Tallow.

"Sicily!" A voice called from the back of the crowd. "Sicily, step away from him!" Ryo pushed his way to the front.

"Papa? What are you doing here? Have you been patrolling with these men? I told you Tal is innocent!" Sicily pointed at the axe in her father's hand, disbelief written on her face. "What were you planning to do with that?"

"Step away from him, Sicily. You don't have to be a part of this. Come with me. We can go home and —."

Sicily stepped back in shock. "I can't believe this! You're taking Lomar's word over that of your own daughter?"

"I'm only thinking of you, Sicily. I'm trying to protect you."

"By robbing me of my inheritance and my future? By pushing me toward a man whom I despise? Are you protecting me from happiness? Is that what this is about? Do you want me to live in misery as you've chosen to do? To make your same mistakes?"

"That's enough! Come with me."

Sicily slowly shook her head. "I never really knew you at all, did I? You certainly don't know me."

She turned her back on her father and moved to Tallow's side. Looking into his eyes, she whispered, "We need to leave—now." Sicily grabbed his hand and pulled. "Run!"

15

It was maddening. Somehow a tinker had recorded the Luminary Navy sending bombs across the limen. The world's governments were asking questions, and the attempt to dismiss it as errant shelling during a military exercise wasn't selling.

The luminary who placed Vigil Strom at this post was not happy. Eli Strom wasn't responsible for the Navy's actions nor the decisions that provoked them, but those facts didn't stop his luminary superiors from blaming him anyway. At this rate, he would never again rise to his former rank.

With growing political demand to grant access to the sky lifts, the Luminaries needed to be seen as benevolent in the event that the tether tribe camps were inspected. Accomplishing that illusion would require a radical change to tether tribe culture. Distasteful as it was to him, Eli needed to become popular among his wards. He also needed to strip away the past as quickly as possible.

Eli was tasked with creating a new kind of tribe at the sky lift encampments. It would mean eliminating mature tribesmen who housed the oral traditions of their past.

It would begin with the formation of new tribes. These would bring together several groups comprised of malleable young men. He anticipated that they would be eager to embrace the many benefits he'd soon bestow upon them. The first change would be the immediate gifting of brides to all men of marrying age. The young tribesmen would have regular access to a new facility already well under construction at the top of one particular sky lift. It would house the spurious wives and children of the new tribes. Tribesmen would no longer be limited to a single conjugal experience. If all went well, the changes would put an altruistic spin on luminary activities regarding the tether tribes.

A figurative and literal fire had been set under these hastily laid out plans. The Luminaries quickly funnelled money into newly created accounts ostensibly filled with tether tribe contributions. It needed to appear as though the luminaries had always been holding tether tribe credits in trust. These funds would be used for the welfare of tether tribe brides in their new homes, something the tribesmen believed was the case all along.

The Luminaries were primarily attempting to mitigate a backlash from foreign governments, but Eli intended to use the changes to forward his own plans to appease one luminary in particular. It was his only hope to redeem himself.

Eli's new plan was to spare the lives of enough older tribesmen to create a few specialized tribes to move into the interior of the swath. A necessary culling would take place, to find the greedy among them. These hand-picked tribesmen would also benefit from Eli's largesse, but they would be tether tribes in name only. The Vigil would shape them into an elite force under his command.

Eli envisioned a specialized group maintaining the traditional tether tribe skills that enabled them to function at the base of the swath. That's where the similarities would end. No longer bound by the fictions of their past, Eli would bind these new tribesmen through their avarice. He would provide a means for the luminary to achieve his goals despite the current setback. As the one in charge of this new force, the luminary would have no choice but to reward him for his efforts.

Eli's elite tribesmen would need to remain isolated, and without local access to a sky lift. He'd already chosen a central location for placement of an unmanned sky lift for his exclusive use. If someone were to inspect it, they would find no encampment at the base. Contrary to established procedure, this sky lift would terminate in the middle of a forested area— seemingly abandoned. It would serve as a dead drop location. Eli would use it for the distribution of his *gifts* as well as his instructions. He could make it work—had to make it work, but first he had to begin the task his superiors had placed on him.

***

Vigil Strom schooled his face to passivity. He watched silently as Flint squirmed in his seat. The primelink was a loose thread and dealing with his incompetence was the first step in Eli's new plan.

The Vigil would need to spend a lot more time at the base of the swath in the foreseeable future, and he needed a temporary base of operations. The primelink's cave would suffice. Fortunately, there would soon be a vacancy.

"You're probably wondering why I wished to speak with you, Primelink Flint."

Flint nodded, uncertain if he was allowed to speak. Curiosity overcame his hesitancy. "I haven't heard anything new from Tallow. I don't believe he will return. He'll no longer be a problem."

He's not the only problem, you fool. The Vigil waved his hand as if it was no longer a concern. "The Luminaries have recognized your efforts and wish to show their gratitude."

Flint sat straighter in anticipation.

"They consider you worthy to receive the first bride among your peers."

Flint beamed. "I'm honoured, Vigil! When will the ceremony take place?"

"I'm afraid there won't be a ceremony."

Flint's face fell. "May I ask why?"

"Don't look so crestfallen, Primelink. The reason is simple. You're to receive a second honour as well—an early hoisting."

Flint looked stunned at first and then elated. "I'm to receive early retirement as well as a bride?"

"Congratulations, Primelink."

"Will there be a ceremony for the hoisting?"

"I'm afraid not, Primelink."

Flint's countenance fell a second time. "How will I be honoured if no one from the tribe bears witness?"

"The Luminaries wish to convey their apologies. Circumstances have arisen creating this unique opportunity for you. A senior primelink from another tribe has died before he could receive his bride," Eli lied. "It's the bride's prerogative to choose another or leave the decision to the Luminaries. This particular bride chose you. You must decide immediately whether you'll accept or she will be granted to another. It's the reason I'm here. The matter carries some urgency."

"What events will follow if I accept?"

"You will be escorted immediately to the sky lift. From there, an honour guard will take you to your bride."

"Right now?" Flint glanced out his cave entrance to the empty campsite. "The tribe has already left for the peat bog. They won't know where I've gone. Am I to be denied the honour in their eyes of both a wife and the hoisting?"

"It's not at all certain when another bride will become available. Others were scheduled before you. It's only because of your recent actions that the Luminaries have decided to grant you this boon. If you were to add insult to injury by rejecting a bride who has specifically chosen you, the Luminaries may be less inclined to consider you favourably in the future."

Flint paled and quickly responded. "Of course, I accept! It's just that— I won't have an opportunity to say goodbye."

Eli mentally rolled his eyes. The man could care less about goodbyes. "You have no need to worry, Primelink. A celebration awaits you at the top of the sky lift. All of your previously hoisted tribesmen will be there to welcome you. The Luminaries themselves will be presiding. What you'd miss here is nothing compared to what awaits."

Flint's eyes sparkled with greed, but he hesitated.

"Never fear, Primelink. I will tell the Blackspike Tether Tribe of the special honour bestowed upon you. I've taken care of everything. An election will occur for your replacement as primelink and you need not worry that it will be Tallow. You've already driven him away. These concerns are beneath you now. It's time for you to rise. What is your decision?"

Flint puffed out his chest. "I'm ready, Vigil."

"Then you leave immediately."

Eli cursed under his breath, placing one foot clip in front of the other as he made his slow way across the ladder bridge leading to the sky lift. Flint had been waiting eagerly for some time when Eli finally arrived.

"How does this work?" Flint asked.

"Clip yourself to the ground tether and make your way to the sky lift. Once you're safely harnessed to the lift, it will begin to ascend."

"You're not coming with me?"

"No, Primelink, this honour is yours and yours alone. I will remain here to witness the hoisting on behalf of your tribe. They will hear of it from my own lips."

Flint's smile grew wide, and he turned to clip himself to the ground tether. Eli heard him whisper. "Finally, I'm getting what I deserve."

Vigil Strom waited until Flint was free of the treeline before he shouted the primelink's words as an epitaph. "It's the time of your hoisting, Primelink! You're finally getting what you deserve!"

Flint turned to smile and wave, just in time to watch the Vigil cut his tether.

16

Screech had turned an ankle while working the peat bog and Bull carried him back to the camp. It was a frustrating waste of his time. The boy needed to learn patience, or one day he'd find himself in freerise.

When they finally arrived back at camp, Bull settled the boy onto his platform to rest, with strict instructions to lay still for the remainder of the day. The camp was generally quiet at mid-morning, so there wasn't much to distract Screech. Bull hoped that would make it easier for the boy to stay put.

At least it should have been quiet, but Bull was surprised to hear a discussion coming from the primelink's cave. He recognized the voices of Flint and Vigil Strom.

Flint had never conducted a secret meeting before—none that Bull was aware of, at least. Curious, he drew near to listen in on the conversation. What he heard was shocking. Vigil Strom was offering Flint the hoisting, but without a goodbye ceremony.

The Vigil's disrespect for their traditions chafed. He'd never been very fond of the Vigil and Bull didn't like the way he manipulated their leader. Something about the Vigil's insistence made Bull suspicious, and he kept his presence hidden.

The entire situation seemed rushed and improper, but Flint seemed willing to accept the Vigil's restrictions. As second in command, it wasn't Bull's place to question Flint's decision. Still, a hoisting without the tribe knowing beforehand—it wasn't right, and Bull decided that if they were denied an opportunity to say their farewells, he could at least stand witness and relate the hoisting to the tribe when they returned.

No one had seen a hoisting before and Bull was uncertain if he would be allowed to observe. *Better not to ask for permission.*

He followed the two men in disbelief. It was happening so quickly. At first Bull wasn't certain how he could make his way to the sky lift without being seen or heard, but Flint went on ahead and Vigil Strom was cursing so loudly as he made his awkward way across the ladder bridges that he was oblivious to Bull's movements.

Bull remained hidden as he observed the sky lift platform. A little thrill washed over him—he was about to witness the hoisting firsthand. On the heels of that thrill came a little wave of guilt, like a child might feel when he's caught doing something he shouldn't. Bull shook the thought away, he was doing this for the tribe as much as himself.

The primelink was halfway across the desert tether on his way to the sky lift when the unthinkable happened. To Bull's shock and great dismay, the Vigil cut Flint's tether. Powerless to help, Bull watched the leader of the Blackspike Tether Tribe hurtle into the ether, trailed by a haunting scream.

It took a great deal of self-control to keep from launching an attack against the Vigil, but circumstances had dramatically changed. This was a very different Vigil than the one he thought he knew. This was an agent of a powerful organization with vast resources, someone who thought nothing of taking a life. If Bull failed to kill the Vigil, or worse, the Vigil killed him, what would be the ramifications for the rest of the tribe? Clearly, the man would have no qualms about killing other potential witnesses. Bull's thoughts turned to Screech lying innocently on his platform. No, it was more important to make sure the tribe was alerted.

He waited in silence as the Vigil reconnected the tether and made his way to the sky lift.

When he was alone, Bull made his way back to the camp. Tallow was right—about everything. Bull hadn't wanted to believe him. He didn't want the change that was coming, but his heritage died along with his leader.

Bull wandered aimlessly through camp for hours. How would the others react when he explained what had happened? Eventually, he found himself in the mouth of Tallow's cave. Bull entered, wishing he could talk to Tallow now. "I'm sorry Tallow, we should have listened." A piece of paper caught his eye, partially covered by the sleeping mat. He bent to retrieve it, imagining he'd see a sketch of Tallow's mysterious Tellusan woman. Instead, he found a map to the stone of witness. Apparently, Flint had missed destroying this one.

Bull walked back to the cave entrance and stared out at the campsite. Melancholy gripped him as he considered leaving it behind. Yet, that's what they would have to do. Tallow's truth had become their own. They needed to leave and live life on their own terms.

Bull glanced at the map in his hand with a new resolve. He wouldn't allow one more tribesman to suffer at the hands of the Luminaries. First thing in the morning, they would leave for the stone of witness.

17

Tallow followed Sicily to her house at the edge of town. She wanted to grab some food and a water skin, anticipating a long and harrowing escape. He was intentionally shortening his stride to accommodate her smaller stature. Diverting to her home seemed a dangerous use of what little time they had, but he was unsure how fast a Tellusan could run. Perhaps it wasn't as much of an issue as he imagined. Besides, he wanted to spend as much time with her as possible before he had to leave her behind.

The thought filled him with anxiety, but he couldn't ask Sicily to risk her life for him. Even so, he wouldn't make that decision until he was out of options. If it became obvious that they would both fall into the clutches of the mob, he would split off from her and draw the pursuers away. Judging by her aggressiveness in the village, it seemed likely that she'd fight for him if she remained at his side. If she did, she might get hurt in the process. That was an unacceptable outcome. He would give his life to prevent that if necessary. Tallow felt certain they wouldn't harm Sicily if she were no longer with him. It was Tallow they wanted.

His only real hope of escape was to make it to the limen before he was caught. Tallow would be in his element and it was unlikely anyone would continue to pursue—Sicily included.

Tallow followed her into her home and watched as she grabbed some dried meat, cheese and bread, stuffing it into a bag. He catalogued her every movement to unpack as a precious memory if he lost her forever.

Sicily searched frantically. "Where did my father leave the water skin?"

Tallow found it hanging from a hook under a coat near the door. "Here it is."

She snatched it from his outstretched hand and ran to the water barrel. It took less than a minute to fill and sling over her shoulder. Those basic needs met, Sicily made a final inspection of the room.

"Do we need to worry about wildlife?" Tallow asked, still imagining a forest filled with carnivores.

Sicily rolled her eyes but grabbed a hunting knife and a rope. "We have more to fear from the darkness. We might not have the luxury of stopping for the night." Sicily grabbed some matches and a lantern which she shoved into Tallow's arms before pushing him out the door. These he stuffed into pockets or clipped to his harness.

A roar sounded from the town square. Sicily cast a worried look at Tallow. "We're out of time." She grabbed Tallow's hand and pulled him toward the field behind the house. "Let's head west. There's another village eighty miles from here. I know it's far, but it's our best option."

One direction was as good as another as far as Tallow was concerned. He needed to find a way to protect them, but was content to follow her lead for now. "Your dreams of travel are coming true, although I don't imagine this is quite what you had in mind."

Sicily cast him a curious look. "This isn't your fault, Tallow." She turned and sprinted in her chosen direction.

Tallow followed a step behind, to create a buffer between her and their pursuers. It would be easier to draw the mob away from the direction Sicily was heading, and hopefully she wouldn't notice until she was a safe distance away.

They were almost to the treeline at the western edge of the field when the mob came flooding around the house. Angry shouts filled the air, and Tallow risked a look over his shoulder to see them pointing in his direction. They'd been spotted and they only had a half-mile lead. Once they entered the treeline, the terrain changed to a mix of forest and clearings for four more miles until the limen.

"We'll make for the limen and then turn west," Sicily shouted. "If they assume you returned to the swath, they might not think to continue west after us."

It was as good a plan as any, but Tallow wasn't willing to take that chance. When they were deep enough into the forest that the villagers couldn't see them, Tallow hung back further, turning abruptly east to head back toward the stone of witness. Tallow picked up speed trying to get as much distance between himself and Sicily as he could to keep her out of harm's way.

Sicily finally realized she couldn't hear Tallow's footsteps behind her any longer. "Tal! What are you doing?" Sicily turned and chased after him.

"Sicily! No! Turn back—keep going."

"I'm staying with you!"

"They're too close, there's no time. We have a better chance if we split up, I'll catch up with you later."

"I'm not losing you again!"

Tallow ran hard, desperate to put more distance between them, but the additional gravity was affecting him. Sicily was moving faster than he expected—as fast as the villagers rapidly closing the distance to the far side of the field. Confusion troubled the mob as they reached the treeline and considered which way they should go. Sicily's suspicions were confirmed when the mob headed straight for the limen. As the two of them continued east instead of west, Tallow realized that her ploy could still work in their favour. The voices faded as Tallow and Sicily fell into a steady jog.

Sicily maintained an angry silence and Tallow left it alone. Survival was the only thing that mattered at the moment and they both knew it.

Tallow wove his way through the trees at an angle toward his destination, hoping to enlarge the search area between the treeline and the limen. It allowed them to continue moving away from the mob while constantly drawing nearer to the swath. If it became necessary, they could turn directly toward the limen. When that time came, Tallow didn't know what would happen. Sicily was matching his stride, and at some point they'd both have to make a decision. *She must have some inkling of what I'm planning.*

It felt strange to move at speed through the trees while running on a large surface. Tallow's arms and legs kept twitching as muscle memory longed to grasp a branch and leap rather than maintain his clumsy loping. It reminded him of those dreams he had where he was fleeing from something terrible but could only move in slow motion—a dream that had become a reality.

Twenty minutes had passed since they last heard any signs of pursuit. Tallow began to think they might actually have a chance at escape. It made him feel a little guilty about trying to leave Sicily behind. He shook his head. *I had no way of knowing how much of a head start we would have. I had to try.*

Sicily stumbled and fell as they descended into a dry creek bed. She took a moment to test her ankle, gingerly putting weight on it as she rose. "I should be fine. Let's keep moving."

They continued on, only a little slower than before. Tallow was reminded of all the things that could go wrong—things out of their control. He prayed fervently that Sicily would be spared if they were caught.

Another fifteen minutes passed and they broke through the clearing at the stone of witness. Both of them were breathing heavily, hands on their knees.

"What were you thinking, dropping back to head off in another direction?" Sicily managed, between gulps of air.

"I was thinking, they're after me and once I'm gone you'll be safe."

"I already told you that I don't need protecting!"

Tallow threw his arms wide in exasperation. "I know that, Sicily, but I can't bear the thought of you getting hurt or worse. Those people have bloodlust in their eyes. It's the same look Flint had when he tried to kill me. You can't reason with people like that—they're uncontrollable. You think you know them, but I thought the same thing of Flint."

"It's not the same—Flint had built up a grudge against you."

"You mean, like Lomar? Do you really know what he's capable of? How far he's willing to go to get what he wants? I know you have your suspicions. And then there's your father—you just told him that you never really knew him. Your circumstances have forever changed, Sicily."

Sicily stared at him in silence for a long minute before nodding. "You obviously had a plan. Care to fill me in?"

"I was going to cross the limen and wait until things settled down. Adis said he would come here in two weeks' time to help if he could. I figured he'd bring you along and we could make plans without a death sentence hanging over our heads."

"You could have told me."

"I didn't have time! The situation unravelled in front of our eyes!"

Sicily sighed. "You have a point. It's a good plan."

"It will only work if you're far from me when the mob arrives. They have to see me crossing the limen without you. If you wait a few days until everyone cools down, you can probably reason with them. You can tell them I abandoned you—make it seem like you're having second thoughts about me. It would give us time to make a plan."

"What if it doesn't work? What if I never see you again?" A tear rolled down Sicily's cheek and Tallow felt his resolve crumbling. He wiped the tear from her face and blinked away the moisture forming in his own eyes.

"It will work, but you have to leave now. Get as far away from me as you can. Take these supplies—I won't need them. Find a safe place to stay and then see if you can catch the tinker alone."

Sicily pulled Tallow into a fierce hug. "I'm so sorry, Tal. This should never have happened. I can't believe the village turned against you before giving you a chance."

Tallow clung to her, inhaling the floral scent of her hair. She felt right in his arms. It couldn't be the end. "It's not your fault. If anyone is to blame, it's Lomar."

As if summoned, Lomar burst into the clearing with two others close behind. "I told you he'd come here!"

Lomar's visage filled with contempt. "Get your hands off of her! Will you never learn?"

Lomar's two friends moved to either side, cutting off any chance of escaping the clearing. They had ugly sneers on their faces and a matching anticipation of violence. *How many people walk around with pleasant smiles to hide a dark heart?* Tallow wondered. Sicily had described the people of Endelton as kind and gentle, but these were not gentlemen. Sicily clearly recognized them and cast a worried glance at Tallow.

"It's too late," Tallow whispered, "There's nowhere for you to run. We'll both have to cross the limen."

Sicily had a terrified expression on her face. "Tal, I can't do that! I don't have the balance to perch on a limb. I'll fall up!"

"I won't let that happen." Tallow held her shoulders at arm's length, to steady her. "You asked me to trust you when I crossed to your side. I'm asking the same thing of you now. I promise—you'll be safe."

Sicily gave a shaky nod of her head.

"I'll hold them off for a moment while you run for the tree bridge. I won't be far behind. When I get there, climb on my back, wrap your arms and legs around my waist and hold tight."

Sicily's eyes widened.

"It's how we travel through the trees while teaching the young."

"I'm a lot bigger than a child!"

"You're forgetting the half gravity. We regularly tote bales of peat a lot heavier than you. Trust me, I can carry you—now go!"

Sicily raced to the tree bridge. Lomar growled and moved to intercept, but Tallow unsheathed the blades of his gauntlets and began swinging. "I'm already a condemned man, I have no reason to hold back this time." Tallow warned.

Lomar stopped his advance and motioned to his friends for support. Each held a long blade and crept closer. Tallow kept a wary eye on the assailant between him and the tree. He made the decision to ignore this threat, and slashed out at the other two who nimbly stepped away from the swing of his blades. While they were still backpedalling, he dropped and spun to face the opponent behind him who had responded by rushing as anticipated. Tallow slashed at the arm thrusting toward him, sending the blade sailing into the brush. The man grabbed his arm and howled in pain, clearing a path to Sicily. Tallow ran without hesitation, pausing only long enough for Sicily to scramble onto his back. He jumped for a stout limb and pulled himself and Sicily up with practised ease. A hand came up to grab his ankle stopping their forward motion before they could get to the limen. Tallow looked down to see Lomar below him. "You're not getting away that easily, tribesman." Lomar began to swing his machete with his free hand, but Tallow sank his boot spurs into Lomar's forearm, forcing him to drop the few feet back to the ground.

Lomar cursed the mother Tallow never knew and pulled himself up onto the tree limb, determined to follow. Tallow and Sicily were already rounding the trunk of the tree, crossing the limen into the swath. Sicily gasped at the sudden shift in gravity and clung tighter, whimpering in fear while Tallow reoriented his feet to the sky. He tied a tether around her wrist and clipped the other end to his harness. "Don't worry, you're attached to me now. I won't let you go." Tallow quickly moved to a higher limb.

Lomar hesitated at the trunk of the tree, but pushed on as he saw his prey moving further away. He reached down to grasp a limb on the swath side and wrapped his arm around it as his legs swung upwards in the reverse gravity. After a few tense moments, he managed to get his footing on another branch and regained his equilibrium. He tested his weight on the branch and sneered. "Moving in the swath isn't so difficult, tribesman. If you thought you were getting away that easily, you'd better think again. I don't have another person on my back to slow me down. You're at a disadvantage, and I'm not stopping until you're dead."

Tallow looked over his shoulder at Sicily. "I'm going to have to jump to the next tree now."

"What? No!"

"It's how we travel in the swath. You've seen me do it before."

"I also saw you cartwheeling into the heavens!"

"I was being careless—experimenting. I won't be trying any risky manoeuvres with you on my back. It's perfectly safe. Close your eyes."

Lomar was nearing their position on the tree. "Return Sicily to me and I might let you go."

"She's not your property to claim, Lomar, and if you think you have a prayer of catching me in my element, you're even less intelligent than I thought."

Lomar growled and lunged as Tallow sprang from the branch. Sicily screamed and then gasped for breath as they reached the apex of Tallow's jump. Another scream escaped as they spanned the final distance to their target, landing with a satisfying thump as the blades sank into bark. Sicily's eyes remained squeezed shut. "Are we dead?"

"If you said something, I didn't hear it. I seem to be deaf in one ear at the moment. Someone was screaming into it."

Sicily opened her eyes and watched as Tallow hammered in a piton and clipped his harness to it. "You see? We're safe. Nothing to it."

"Nothing to it? I'm going to be swallowing for hours trying to get my heart back down where it belongs."

Tallow rounded the trunk so they could get a better view of Lomar. He had to give up now. They'd wait until he crossed back over the limen and then they could discuss next steps.

Lomar jumped from one branch to another, testing his new environment.

"What's he doing?" Sicily wondered aloud.

"He wouldn't!" Tallow exclaimed. "Hang on, we need to jump again." Tallow didn't wait for an answer. Mercifully, Sicily didn't scream in his ear again. They reached the next tree and rounded the trunk in time to see Lomar crouching. "Lomar, don't be a fool! It's too dangerous!"

Lomar ignored him and launched toward the tree they had just vacated. Unfortunately, he did what anyone under full gravity would do and pushed as hard as he could to guarantee his momentum. In half gravity, it was an overcompensation that bounced him off his intended target and sent him spinning through the treetops. He didn't even see the heavy limb that connected with his skull, knocking him unconscious.

Tallow made three desperate dives in an attempt to catch him, but Lomar was moving too quickly, and as he had so gleefully noted, Tallow had another person on his back. Unfortunately, Lomar's imagined advantage turned out to be his own handicap.

Tallow slowly shook his head in a state of shock at the hatred that would drive a man to such madness. His eyes followed Lomar until his unconscious form cleared the treetops. Then, Tallow turned to the horrified men who had watched it unfold from the other side of the limen. "You are witnesses!" He yelled. "Lomar died of his own foolishness and not by my hand. If you had listened to Sicily or the tinker instead of a cruel and greedy man like Lomar, none of this would have happened. Go home and tell the others what you've seen. You got your wish—I'm leaving."

"Now what?" Sicily asked as the two men returned to the village.

"Now you learn to become comfortable with your new mode of travel." Without waiting for her to answer, Tallow leaped for another tree, and then two more for good measure.

Sicily screamed in his other ear.

18

Today was the day that Adis, the tinker, was due to return to the stone of witness. It had been a busy and surprising two weeks. Bull had arrived at their makeshift campsite with one of Tallow's maps in hand. Tallow recalled the moment when Bull read the stone of witness and angrily crushed the map he was holding. In an unexpected turn of events, Bull had experienced something similar to that of the man who engraved the stone, rejecting what he had previously believed and embracing the truth inscribed on the stone.

Not everyone in the tribe was ready to face the prospect of crossing the limen, but they were in unanimous agreement that they needed to live life on their own terms and in new ways.

The tribe had set up camp near the stone of witness, and Tallow enjoyed the companionship of his brothers while familiarizing them with different methods for crossing the limen. Tallow had learned he could easily leap across from the ground as long as he could find a tree within jumping distance on the swath side of the limen. The tree bridge was still a good first step for leery initiates, but depending on where they chose to live, that might not be available to them.

Sicily was sitting on the grass explaining the vagaries of life as a

Tellusan. Her audience walked and leaped about, familiarizing themselves with the effects of full gravity as they considered her advice.

Adis arrived with a bemused smile on his face as he took in the scene. "Greetings," he called out, drawing the eyes of everyone within earshot. The tribesmen knew Tallow was expecting a visitor, but remained on edge until he assured them that this was indeed the man he had been waiting for. As Tallow approached the tinker with Bull in tow, he noticed that Adis had arrived with two mounts that he was busy tying to trees at the edge of the clearing.

Tallow embraced the tinker as a brother and encouraged Bull to do the same. "I'm very happy to see you." Tallow grinned.

"Nowhere near as glad as I am to see both you and Sicily alive and well. Who are your friends, if I may ask?"

"These are my brothers, who have learned the truth about the Luminaries." Tallow filled Adis in on the events leading to the death of Flint and the exodus of the tribe.

"It saddens me that your primelink learned the truth too late, but I'm pleased that no more of your tribe will suffer that fate."

Bull bowed his head to the tinker in gratitude.

Adis considered the bustling glade and directed his next question to Bull. "Does the tribe have plans for the future?"

"Well," Bull began, "A number of us are willing to consider leaving the swath permanently, but the idea of abandoning everything we know, is frightening. Starting over is a difficult consideration for members of the tribe. Many are content with our lifestyle."

"I can understand their hesitation. It's a lot to take in. What will you do?"

Tallow was as curious about Bull's response as the tinker was. He'd been so caught up in the joy of their reunion, he hadn't thought to ask.

"We're considering a staged approach. It occurred to us that we could build a campsite that crosses the limen. We envision constructing an enclosed bridge to make the passage across the limen a safe and reliable one. Then we can take our time gaining confidence in this new world, knowing home and family are always nearby."

"A sensible strategy. Have you given any thought to a location?"

"We were hoping for some advice in that regard. From what Tallow has told me, this location isn't safe for us. However, we would like to settle within a reasonable distance of a Tellusan village. Given time, we feel we might have items we could offer in trade, to build a rapport. We've learned how to make very light yet strong tethers and can offer other items or services that may hold some value. Who knows? Perhaps over time, some Tellusans may become intrigued by life in the swath and join our hybrid village."

"A plan both ambitious and worthy! I know of a village that may suit your needs. It's at the farthest reach of my circuit, I'm afraid. Remote as it is, the citizens rely equally on foraging and harvesting for survival. I believe you'd have a great deal to offer them. They also have a dubious distinction that may play in your favour."

Sicily had walked over to give Adis a hug and join the conversation, "Dubious distinction? What might that be?"

"The population of that town has a ratio of two women for every man," Adis smiled. "You never know, some of you may find a wife if you can prove your worth."

Bull's eyebrows rose. "It sounds like a place that may give an outsider a chance."

"I'll be back that way in a month's time. I'll draw you a map and you can start your journey while I complete my route. It will give you time to set up camp. When I arrive, I can make introductions."

"That's very generous of you."

"The village is called Swiftwater. It sits along the banks of the second river you will cross if you continue west along the limen. The town is a week's journey from here. Once you arrive at the river, it can be found less than three miles south of the swath. When you arrive, I suggest you quietly scout out the town to make sure you have the correct location.

Cut a notch beneath the lower limb of a tree close to the river where it crosses the limen and on other trees as you move in the direction of your new settlement. I'll follow those when I come looking for you."

Sicily glanced at Tallow. "Maybe we should go with them."

"Perhaps." Tallow looked at the ground where he was moving a pebble back and forth with his foot.

"Tal?"

"I want to start a new life with you, Sicily, and I intend to. It's just that so many other tether tribes don't know what the Luminaries are doing to them. I feel torn by a sense of obligation to you and them both."

"Actually," Adis interrupted, "I have a proposal that may help."

Tallow and Sicily both waited for Adis to continue. Sicily spoke first. "Well? What's your proposal?"

"Oh, I'm sorry, I thought you two had more to discuss. Yes, well," Adis cleared his throat. "The Tinker's Guild sees an opportunity to have eyes and ears on luminary activity within the swath. That is, if you are willing to serve in that capacity, Tallow. You would spend most of your time in Tellus and part in the swath on scouting missions for the Guild. It would allow you to seek out tribes and work at extracting them from luminary influence."

Adis scratched his jaw as he considered further. "Hmmm, this could work out better than I originally imagined. If the Blackspike Tether tribe is successful at setting up a permanent residence, they could provide a point of transition for other tribes who decide to cross the limen. Swiftwater might indeed be a good home base for the two of you. Unfortunately, what the Guild has in mind would require a lot of travelling."

Sicily sprouted an eager grin and slapped Tallow's arm. "Did you hear that Tal? Lots of travel!"

Tallow chuckled at Sicily's expression.

"That sounds great, Adis, but we're in the same position as when this all began. Tal and I have no money, no means of transportation, and no way to travel safely.”

“You do now.” Adis motioned toward the animals.

Sicily laughed. “What, you’re giving us mounts?”

“And substantial funds to get a start in your new life.”

“I was joking, Adis. That’s very generous, but we can’t accept those rides from you.”

“Oh—they’re not from me.”

Sicily shot a questioning look at Tallow, who appeared equally confused.

“As you know, the Tinker’s Guild provides legal services for remote settlements. As it happens, Lomar Romero has no living relatives. Since he has no heir to claim his estate, it falls on me to decide how to distribute his assets. I’ve decided two of his mounts as well as the gold in the saddlebags should go to you as recompense for your suffering.”

Adis wasn’t finished. “You mentioned a concern about safety when travelling. As retainers for the Guild, you can approach any tinker to request an escort at no charge. Also, the Guild will provide a small stipend for your services. It’s not much, but it’s enough to live on.”

Tallow was overwhelmed. “I don’t know what to say.”

Adis smiled. “Say yes.”

“What do you think, Sicily?”

“Are you kidding? Startup funds and ongoing opportunities to travel with an armed escort? Tal, that’s a life generally reserved only for the very wealthy. Plus you can help other tether tribes in ways you wouldn’t consider on your own. I vote yes.”

Tallow grinned, succumbing to her infectious excitement. “Then I say yes.”

Adis brought his hands together in a single loud clap. “Excellent! I’ll have the papers drawn up. You can travel with me or remain in Swiftwater until the Guild has a specific task.”

Tallow noticed that Sicily had stopped smiling. “Is something wrong?”

"I'm still angry with my father, but I can't stop worrying what will become of him when I'm gone."

"Did I forget to mention? While I was going over the estate ledgers, I discovered that Lomar owned the gambling establishment. Can you imagine? The man took advantage of your father's gambling addiction to lay claim to your family property. I've forgiven your father's debt and returned the title of the homestead to him. I've distributed the remainder of the estate to Endelton as communal property to benefit its citizens. Lomar's home will provide room and board for travellers or villagers who find themselves without shelter. The needy will also have access to the produce from that land. As a condition of this disbursement, the gambling house will remain closed. Mayor Hawton agrees that it was a source of many problems. Unless your father has the means to travel, it's unlikely he'll be able to feed his gambling habit. He should be able to hold on to the farm."

Sicily hugged herself as a tear slid down her cheek. Then she hugged Adis. "I can't thank you enough." She whispered.

Adis patted her on the back. "Your gratitude is unnecessary. The disbursement of Lomar's estate was a welcome opportunity for justice. It brought me a great deal of pleasure to enact it."

The three of them looked at each other with grateful smiles. Tallow broke the silence first. "Well, then, I guess we have a future to plan for."

"There's just one other thing we need to take care of—a small legal matter. If Tallow is going to work for the Guild under the authority of the government, he needs to become a citizen of the Southern Kingdom."

Adis rifled through his bag and pulled out some documents. "For starters, you'll need to sign these papers with your first and surname."

Tallow looked at Sicily in confusion.

"Adis, Tal doesn't have a last name."

Adis grinned. "I guess he'll just have to take yours. Then there's the matter of a long overdue ceremony."

Tallow and Sicily began to laugh as Adis's suggestion sank in.

"I'll need you to sign here as well, Sicily."

Tallow didn't hear anything else that the tinker said. He was too busy gathering his brothers to share in his joy and stand witness to the first public marriage ceremony ever held in the presence of an entire tether tribe, one which he dearly hoped would be the first of many.

States of Inversion

Grasping at Gravity is a standalone novella set in the *States of Inversion* universe.

The novella takes place in an isolated location, offering a taste of the broader world surrounding it.

The Tinker's Guild plays an important role in the political machinations of the various global factions, but there is so much more to explore about life on a planet fractured by a strip of reversed half gravity. The floating cities of the Luminaries maintain their vantage from within the swath, hemmed in by the Unified Northern Collective and the monarchy of the Southern Lands. Each fights to maintain a precarious truce, suspicion heightening tension.

Through it all, the question remains about the origin of the swath. What is its mysterious purpose, and how are the Iridogen connected to it all? I hope you'll come along for the ride.

If you enjoyed this novella, please consider leaving a review.

If you would like to receive updates about my progress on the series, along with limited offers and exclusive content, consider visiting my website to join the mailing list. I don't send newsletters out very often, so you don't have to worry about me filling your inbox.

All the best,
Kallen Samuels
https://www.kallensamuels.com/